Also from Second Wind Publishing
by George Wright

The Runaway and *Flyswatter* in one volume
America Reborn
Redstone

Yaweta

By

George Wright

Savage Books

Published by Second Wind Publishing

Kernersville

Savage Books
Second Wind Publishing, LLC
931-B South Main Street, Box 145
Kernersville, NC 27284

First Savage Books edition published September, 2008.
Savage Books, Running Angel, and all production design are trademarks of Second Wind Publishing, used under license.

For information regarding bulk purchases of this book, digital purchase and special discounts, please contact the publisher at www.secondwindpublishing.com

Cover design by LeJoy Rothe

Manufactured in the United States of America

ISBN 978-1-935171-03-4

To my son, Ross Wright.

—George Wright

PREFACE

Before you start reading this story, you need to understand that it takes place a hundred years or more before Christopher Columbus made his epic journey in 1492. The word, "Indian", to describe the inhabitants of North America, had not yet been invented. Most of the various tribes were not called by the names they have today. Buffalo, or the American Bison, had not been named. The various native tribes had names for trees, rivers, and mountains but none of these carry the names now that they had then. In many instances I have used the modern names only for the better understanding of the story. What is called a, "deer" in the United States is (or was) called a, "hart" or a, "roe deer" in Europe. What is called an "elk" was commonly called a, "deer" in the old country and a, "moose", was an, "elk". When I refer to animals, some trees and some native tribes I may use the modern name, but that should not distract the reader from the story. In that time Ireland was called, "Erin".

1.
SEAN O'CONNELL

Before the North American continent was "discovered", and before any of the lakes, rivers, and landmarks were named by anyone other than the natives, men of adventure came to the shores of the continent. Sean O'Connell, an Irishman, was one of those adventurers.

Sean O'Connell was big for his age and always in trouble. As is so typical of highly intelligent children, he was bored with the normal activities of daily life and sought other outlets for his energy. The son of a wealthy jeweler in Dublin, he had completed his education and was serving his apprenticeship so he could follow in his father's footsteps. His father had honored him by changing the sign in front of the store to read, "O'Connell and Son". This was done because the boy had demonstrated tremendous skill in the making of fine jewelry.

The English were occupying his homeland at the time. They thought they ruled Ireland, but no true Irishman would acknowledge the claim. Part of his father's pride in his son was the boy's skill at harassing the enemy. The guerilla activities of Mister O'Connell and his son were well known to their countrymen and suspected by the English. Sean's father had a reputation as a patriot and leader of the rebellion. Sean was not considered a suspect because of his age.

On the second day of June, during his twelfth year, Sean's life changed forever. His father was making a broach in the back of the store, on a special order. Sean's mother was taking care of the front counter. Sean was out making a delivery and was to stop by another customer's home to help design a special ring.

Three young English officers came into the store. They had been drinking but were quite polite at first, saying they were looking for jewelry for their wives. The O'Connell's didn't like doing business with the enemy, but business being what it was, there was no choice. Sean's mother was very cool toward them, trying to be cordial and all business. She was a beautiful young woman and the men began to flirt with her. When she rejected their advances they became more insistent. As she handed one of them a ring he had asked to see he grabbed her hand and would not let go.

Most of the Officers in the English Army were the sons of the Nobility. Those of higher rink were from the upper class, but those of low rank were generally from lesser Nobility. Most of them were fine men, with high morals, and high standards but some of those of lower rank were the rich, arrogant, spoiled sons that were in the military because their family thought they just might learn to be men. The two Officers that entered the store were of the latter sort.

She called to her husband and tried to pull away but was grabbed by the other two and yanked over the counter. Her scream of terror brought the elder O'Connell from the back room. One of the men was holding his wife while another was ripping at her clothing. O'Connell picked up a knife and charged. He managed to kill one of the officers but he was stabbed by the others. He lay mortally wounded and bound as his wife was repeatedly raped and then murdered. When they were through with their entertainment they slit the jeweler's throat.

As Sean was returning from his errands he saw the drunken English officers leaving the store. They were laughing and straightening up their clothes. After discovering the carnage Sean reported the incident and pointed out the two officers he had seen. He was thrown in jail for daring to accuse two officers of the Crown of such a hideous crime. Six citizens of Dublin were rounded up, charged, and executed for killing the officer Sean's father had killed. The rape and murder of Sean's parents was not even mentioned.

Sean spent the next year learning how to be tough. He learned quickly. Prison was a matter of the survival of the fittest and Sean was as fit as they came. He learned that there was only one way to win a fight - any way you can. There was no such thing as a fair fight, only winners. He was always big for his age, muscular, quick, and a fast learner. In prison he learned to be hard. By the end of that first year Sean was the leader of a massive jailbreak, killing three guards with his bare hands.

His hatred for the enemy soon caused them to wish they had put him to death instead of just throwing him in prison. Sean learned, as no one had ever learned, how to survive on the streets. He learned the art of stalking his enemy and moving about silently without being seen. On his fifteenth birthday he gave himself a present.

Two English soldiers had a girl Sean's age against a stone wall. In spite of her screams for help they ripped off her clothing, leaving her standing as naked as the day she was born. Several men ran to help her, Sean included. This type of harassment was common and seemed to be considered good sport by some of the soldiers. Any retaliation by the townsmen would be punished by death or prison so they went to the girl and covered her body. They took her home crying. Sean recognized the two officers as the same ones who had murdered his parents. He followed them.

For three more hours the two walked the streets, having a great time. They stopped frequently and drank from their bottles. They accosted every female they met, ripping at their clothing to expose them or just grabbing at their private areas. Eventually the two men had a feeling they were being followed. Every time they looked there was no one behind them. This was probably true. Sean was not always behind them. He was beside them, ahead of them, and all around them, but seldom behind them.

Late in the afternoon they tired of revelry and playing their game. They decided it was time to get serious. They chose for their target an eleven-year-old girl playing with a doll. They rapped her over the head, knocking her unconscious, and carried her to a lonely place in some nearby trees. This was Sean's opportunity. They were away from prying eyes. The two soldiers were enjoying themselves by removing the girls clothing piece by piece and laughing in anticipation. When the girl was completely naked they decided to have a race in their own disrobing to see who would have her first. Both men were almost out of their uniforms when Sean struck. With their breeches around their knees they did not have much of a chance. Sean stepped between them. A hard right to the left temple of one and an equally hard left to the right temple of the other put them out.

When the two officers regained their senses each was tied between two trees. Their arms and legs were spread apart as far as possible, and their feet were off the ground. They were spread-eagled in the air, stark naked. Sean was busy putting the unconscious girl's clothing back on her small body. When he was finished he picked her up and carried her home. She regained her senses back where she had been kidnapped, with her doll in her arms. She never knew what had happened.

11

When Sean O'Connell returned, the two officers recognized him and knew they were in a little trouble. They soon discovered how vindictive a young boy can be. The officers who raped Sean's mother and killed his dad soon felt the young man's wrath and paid for their crimes. Sean went from man to man; removing parts and forcing them into their mouths. Eventually they bled to death but not before a great deal of suffering. He left them hanging where they were.

The next morning an arrow killed the commander of the detachment stationed in the area. He was a hard, cruel man who was not liked very much even by the men in his command. It happened to be the same man that had thrown Sean in prison. A note attached to the arrow told where the two mutilated officers were, how they died, why, and who did it. The two he had tortured were the only sons of two royal families. Sean was automatically a condemned man but he would have to be caught before they could execute him.

He was like a shadow, always there, but disappearing when the light hit him. He was supported by his many friends, eating in their homes and given whatever he wanted. No one knew where he slept. He changed those quarters frequently and always made sure they were well hidden. He spent full time killing the enemies of his native land. Although many offered to join him he always worked alone. In prison he had learned to trust no one and it was easier to hide by himself.

He became known as, "the Ghost". When the soldiers avoided an area because the Ghost was making it too dangerous, Sean changed areas. When the soldiers were sent in force, Sean disappeared. Eventually he had to go into the army's camp to find targets. When the soldiers ventured out they traveled in groups of five or six. Even then many died because an arrow had come out of the darkness. People were tortured and large bribes were offered but no one really knew where the Ghost would be at any particular time. Most of the Irish would rather die than betray him anyway. Some did.

It was slightly over a year before Sean, the Ghost, was almost caught. Seven burly soldiers jumped him with clubs. Their mission was to bring him in alive for a public hanging. Sean fought for his life. The first blows stunned him momentarily but caused him to lose his temper. With a dagger in each hand he lashed out in all directions. Beaten and bruised, he finally got away. Two soldiers were dead and three were badly wounded. A house-to-house search was made to find him but the wounded boy was secretly shifted from hiding place to hiding place. The soldiers had orders to kill. He was wanted, not dead or alive, just dead!

A ship, the Dame Mary, was in harbor at a city on the seaward side of the island country. Sean was smuggled across the country and brought aboard. The captain was a Scot named MacGregor who happened to be a friend of Sean's father. Captain Mac, as he was nicknamed and his Scottish crew had no more love for the English than Sean did. The ship sailed that very night leaving the cargo they were supposed to load sitting on the dock. When this was discovered the Dame Mary was declared a privateer and a war ship was sent in pursuit.

At seventeen Sean soon became an able seaman. He remembered Captain Mac as a frequent visitor in his father's home. The warm memories of the captain helped in his transition. He refused the job of Cabin Boy and insisted on the post of Able Seaman. He took on the hardest jobs and delighted in trying to outwork the older, more experienced, men. His eagerness to learn and easy manner soon made him an accepted member of the crew.

Sean became quite close to one member of the crew. He was younger by several years than his shipmates were and much closer to Sean's age. He was the odd one of the group. His name was not Gaelic, it was, "Sven". He was bigger than the others and the only one who could come close to Sean's strength. Sean discovered he had a Scottish mother, a Norse father, and a very rough childhood. They entertained each other with tales of their youth.

The ship sailed west and south with a war ship right behind. The Dame Mary was lighter but the English ship had more sail. One could not out-run the other. The Ships sailed for many days, intent on their assigned missions. An Atlantic storm put a stop to the chase.

A sudden squall arose. High waves tossed the small ship like a matchstick in rapids. The larger English ship, being less affected by the rough seas, drew close. The smaller ship prepared for battle as the storm grew stronger. The intensity of the storm became such that each ship had to concentrate on staying afloat. The ships began to drift apart. In time the English ship was nowhere in sight.

When the storm subsided, the forward mast was broken and they had lost the capacity to steer. The seas were still rough with a steady wind blowing the Dame Mary farther west. When the seas finally became calm the crew made a temporary repair to the rudder so the ship could be steered but they had been in unfamiliar waters for a long time. Fresh water had to be rationed and there was no food on board when the lookout sighted land. The ship came close to shore and dropped anchor. Then they took the lifeboats and went ashore to hunt, replenish their fresh water, cut a tree to replace the mast, and undertake the many repairs. The projects would take several days of hard work. They thought they had come to a large island.

It was a beautiful land, thickly wooded with plenty of game for food. The landing boats beached on a smooth sandy area. A few yards back the forest began. As they came close to the shore one of the men spotted a deer. He killed it with an arrow from his long bow. The crew would eat well for the first time in weeks. With the ship securely anchored the entire crew came ashore. With Sean, Captain Mac, and the crew, there were eighteen of them. They finished the deer in one meal.

It was a strange new land. They met no native population so considered the island unoccupied. Captain Mac saw the commercial value of the timber and game immediately. They decided to farther explore the land. When repairs were completed and they could once again navigate, they sailed into a large bay and up a big river. Several days later they came to a lake. After sailing around the shoreline they arrived at the southwest end of the lake and went ashore.

Winter caught them. Captain Mac was all too familiar with the storms of the North Atlantic in winter. By the time they cut a shipload of timber and loaded it, they would be in the middle of the worst part of the year. Their small ship would need better sailing conditions with a heavy load. He decided they could spend the winter on the ship, anchored close to shore. During the winter and spring they would cut enough timber to make a cargo. This way it would be possible to sail in the late spring or early summer when conditions were at their best. With a cargo so valuable they could probably buy their way out of any trouble. Naturally Sean would not return with them. No amount of money would buy his life.

2.
YAWETA

As they were coming up the river there had been several sightings of natives, or something, along the shoreline. No one was ever certain of what they had seen because all they ever had was a fleeting glimpse. Now things were different. Natives were in the area. When hunting parties went out there were signs of them, and occasionally one would be seen. Three different times arrows had hit the armor of the hunters and bounced off. One man came in with an arrow in his arm. The Indian arrowheads were of flint rather than the hard, sharp steel the Europeans used and were not effective against the armor the men wore. When the Indians saw arrows bounce from the sailors' chests it frightened them. The strange vessel in the lake and the strange-looking white braves with hair on the face were new to the natives. Since they would not die when hit with arrows the natives left them alone.

All was well until the lake froze over. There was a long cold spell and the ice became thicker every day. Finally the pressure of the ice around the ship cracked the hull like the shell of an egg. Water came into the lower portions of the ship, causing the men to abandon that area. Eventually, large sections of the hull began to drift away under the ice. There was no danger of sinking because the ice formed under the upper part. It would be impossible to salvage the ship once the ice melted. Knowing this, they were well prepared when the ship began to sink. They saved everything they could, including the ship's long boat, and went ashore before anyone was endangered.

In exploring the region they went up a river to a great falls. A little farther on could be seen another lake. It looked as though they had found another ocean, but after arriving at the new body of water, it was fresh, not salt. They carried the long boat overland and launched it to explore the shoreline. Their boat was large enough for them but not for all their supplies, so they built a large raft to pull along behind the boat. What they thought would be a short trip of a week or so turned into a journey of several months.

They traveled from one lake, through a channel, into another. Four months later they had explored four large lakes. The lakes were more like inland seas, so big they could not see the far shore. When they finally stopped they had come to a stretch of land that came out into the lake forming a cove. A river entered the lake at the head of the cove. It was a good sheltered area, and their second winter was starting.

When they came ashore to build shelters for the winter and to gather food for the coming months, they met the first Indians they had ever seen up close. The meeting was equally traumatic for both parties. The sailors had never met natives other than at a distance, and the natives had never seen white men. There was a cautious meeting, neither trusting the other nor yet neither wanting to start a war. With sign language and great difficulty they communicated. The Indians had been watching them for months. They had been afraid to show themselves, not knowing what the men with hair on their faces and white skin wanted in the land.

Many of the sailors had armor and helmets, which they wore to shore. The natives were fascinated with the hard shell. Some ran away when the men started to remove their armor.

The first meeting of white and red men was peaceful and trading began. Steel knives were traded for furs and food. As best as the men could understand, the natives called themselves "The People". When the natives asked the name of the men's tribe, Captain Mac told them they were from the Mary Dame. He had inadvertently reversed the name of the ship, but didn't bother to correct the error. The natives did not understand the words but tried to remember them. As time went on they had a workable name. As far as the natives were concerned, the men were, "Mandan". The natives and the explorers spent the winter together.

Never had the natives seen any man as big as Sean. He was over head taller than any other man in the party was. His armor had been specially made by the ship's blacksmith. Because of his size regular armor would not fit him. The sword the blacksmith made was larger than ordinary. Sean had grown and become a man by now. At eighteen he was (in today's measurements) six feet eight inches tall and weighed two hundred and fifty pounds. He had broad muscular shoulders and looked slim in the waist. Both arms and legs were corded with muscle. His youth prevented him from having much of a beard but the sun had darkened his skin to a copper colored brown that seemed to be trying to match his dark red hair. He was one of those men with a lot of body hair on his chest, arms, and legs. This was something entirely new to the people he now knew. Actually his body was only a shade lighter than that of the Indians. Like many truly big men he was very good-natured and outwardly friendly so when he was treated as somewhat of a phenomenon he took it as a complement. Children followed him around because of his kindness toward them. Women eyed him, and most warriors were either jealous or afraid of him. He learned their language quickly and the meaning of the sign language.

As the men stayed in the village, nature took its usual course. By spring most of the Scots had Indian wives. Sean was shy around the fair sex, so he never took a bride. He was offered a wife several times by fathers but each time he was able to persuade the father to let the girl marry a brave who had eyes for her. His main interest was the native way of life.

When the Indians played, they played at war and survival. The men from the ship demonstrated their prowess with the longbow, spears, and swords. The swords were fascinating to the braves. Never had they seen such an instrument. Steel was unknown to the natives, who used flint knives and tomahawks made of stone. The longbow of the ship's crew had a longer range than the shorter bow of the natives, but the natives were much more accurate. The steel points of the spear might have been better, but the natives had more skill.

Sean was especially popular with his demonstrations of strength and skill. With the larger-than-normal sword he could fell a tree a full hand's width in diameter with a single blow. He could throw his knife farther and more accurately than his fellows could. When it came to the longbow he had no equal. There were contests of skill that Sean began to win with regularity. When it came to the wrestling games Sean was in his element, having had a lot of practice during his youth.

The next spring Sean earned a native name and gained a companion. The snow had been gone for nearly a month, and the natives were preparing to move camp. One of the children, an orphan boy of about ten summers, who lived with various members of the tribe, was missing. He had wandered out of the camp. Sean went to find him. When the lad was found he was crouched against the roots of a fallen tree with a mountain lion cub clutched in his arms.

The boy was frozen in fright, unable to move. The cub's mother had him cornered and was about to leap when Sean came upon the scene. Sean distracted the lioness and worked his way between her and the boy. She charged, leaping for his throat. Being unarmed Sean caught the cat in his big hands. One hand gripped inside the cat's mouth and around the lower jaw. His other hand held one of the cat's back legs. A paw raked across his shoulder, cutting deep. Another ripped down his chest. Sean knelt down and broke the animal's back over his knee. Next, he twisted the cat's head around and broke its neck. He threw the dead cat as far as he could, picked up the frightened boy, and returned to camp. Blood ran down his arm and chest.

Sean's wounds were dressed by the ship's doctor. He would carry the scars for the rest of his life. When the boy told the story there was a great celebration. Sean was begged to tell the story himself, but modesty prevented him. It was the custom of the Indians to brag about their exploits around the fire, so the boy did the bragging for him. From that day forward he was known as "Yaweta", which loosely translated would mean, "The Giant Protector of the People". In a solemn ceremony, he was adopted into the tribe as blood brother to the chief. Since the boy had no family Sean adopted him. The boy was called, "He Who Has No One" so Yaweta gave him a new name. From then on he would be called "Sojata" - Son of the Giant.

With his new status in the tribe Sean was given a new tepee when they arrived at the new campground. Because of his size, and his new son, his tepee needed to be quite large. Tradition held that no tepee could be larger than that of the chief. To solve this problem Sean picked

20

a place about a hundred yards away down in a secluded part of the forest. Sean and his son soon became very close.

The new camp was hard against a great plain. For the first time the sailors saw the animal that was of great value to native life. It was a large animal built somewhat like a cow but with a large shaggy head and small horns. The front shoulders were large and covered with shaggy fur. There was a hump above the front shoulders and the body then tapered back to a rear that was small in comparison and almost bare of fur. Overall it was one ugly animal. The plains were black with their numbers in great herds reaching from horizon to horizon. The native name for the animal could only be translated as, "Food of Life", but in later years the animal would be called the American Bison, or the Buffalo. During the summer, they learned how to creep up on the animals close enough to kill them with bow and arrow. Sean learned how to get close enough to use his sword on them. Before the animals would run away Sean could usually get two or three. His newly acquired skill made him very popular with the tribe.

The hunt lasted until the natives had acquired all they needed for the coming year. There was no waste. The natives used every part of the animal. It made meat, needles, thread, clothes, and almost everything the natives needed. They even used the dung. It made good firewood for their campfires. All this time Sean was learning.

When the weather started to change, the tribe moved back to their original location. By spring, Sean was the only unmarried member of the original ship's company. Captain Mac married the chief's daughter. From the first the captain was recognized as the chief of the crew. The men obeyed his orders and looked to him for guidance. Every marriage had been conducted with him reciting words after the chief had performed the native ceremony. It was, therefore, appropriate for him to marry the beautiful daughter of the tribal chief. The celebration lasted a full week.

The chief of the white warriors had always submitted himself to the authority of the other chief but there were actually two tribes living in the one camp. The captain knew this might eventually cause problems so he called a meeting of the ship's crew. The natives called them Mandan, which the men took to mean, "White Natives", so this is the name they claimed. Captain Mac was called Chief Mac by his crew. They used the native's word for chief.

They no longer had a ship and did not have the tools necessary to build an ocean-going vessel. Even if they could get home, unless they had a rich cargo, they were sure to hang because they had helped Sean get away. None of the men had close relatives or other ties across the Atlantic. Since they had already started a new life, it was an easy decision to stay in the new land. They decided to form their own tribe. The cultural differences between them and the Indians could be a problem. They decided to take their families west to find the western coast of the island. There, they would establish a new home where they could start their own culture and traditions. Captain Mac was sure the western coast would be just the other side of the plain where they had camped during the summer.

The captain and his navigator drew a map showing the river they had traveled and the lakes they had explored in the middle of a big island. The coasts of the island could only be a few days' travel to the west, south and north in their estimation so the map was drawn with this in mind. Back home they had heard tales of a land to the west but they had also heard tales of dragons in the waters of the ocean. They felt they had disproved the dragons but had found the land.

Preparations were made and three days later all but Sean had departed. He decided to become an explorer and travel over the land. His findings would be reported back to the captain and the map adjusted accordingly. He decided to go south and find the southern coast. Then he would follow it around and meet up with his friends on the western coast later. It was not a bad plan, considering the assumptions they had made.

A week passed. Sean departed from the tribe. The Indians had not only taught him their language but the art of talking in signs. Yaweta had learned all the ways of the tribe. His son Sojata was with him to help in the journey. He had been told of other tribes who were not friendly, might try to harm him, so he was cautious, and traveled in his armor. Sean decided to use his new name. Other tribes, he was assured, would be more apt to recognize it and understand what it meant. He was starting a new life so he decided his new name would be appropriate.

They had been traveling in a southwest direction for several days. In the late afternoon camp was set up beside a small river, and Yaweta went hunting for food. Sojata stayed in camp, preparing it for the night. Yaweta had not gone far when he was set upon by natives. A war party of thirty braves was on their way to raid another tribe. Three of the braves were scouting ahead of the rest when they spotted Yaweta. They hid themselves and lay waiting.

An arrow came out of nowhere, bouncing off his breastplate. Two more arrows barely missed him. Then three Indians charged with tomahawks. One of the braves landed a blow to Yaweta's head. It bounced off his helmet, doing no harm. Reluctantly he drew his sword and quickly dispatched two of his attackers. In a single swipe of the big sword one was decapitated and the other's chest was opened. The third man ran back to the main party.

Minutes later the air was full of arrows and spears. Several of the missiles found their mark. His arms and legs were nicked, but his armor protected him from any real harm. He charged the war party with sword in hand. The Indians had never seen a sword, a white man, or any man close to the size of Yaweta. As the arrows bounced from his armor several ran in fright. By the time the conflict was over fully half the war party was dead. All the rest had fled in disarray.

Sojata dressed Yaweta's wounds. He had watched as Yaweta fought the attackers. There would be no more trouble with that tribe for a while.

When the survivors of the war party returned to their village, they told the story. In their eyes, they had fought with a god of war. There was no exaggeration when they told the story but many in the tribe went away in disbelief. In their eyes a warrior who could not be killed and laughed at arrows could not exist. The strange weapon, his size, and description were all unbelievable. Yet the story spread from village to village.

The duo continued toward the southwest until they came to a large river, flowing from northwest toward the southeast. A trail led along the bank. They chose to go southeast and follow the river to its mouth. As they walked along they came to a village. They had walked right up to the very village of the raiding party he had been forced to fight.

By the time Yaweta saw the village he knew they had seen him. They stopped as several braves appeared around them. They made no hostile move but Yaweta was taking no chances. With Sojata behind him he walked toward the settlement. He recognized the dress of the Indians as the same as the ones he had killed but did not know they were of the same village. More people appeared along the side of the path as he came closer. Squaws, children, and braves stood watching in silence. At the center of the village he could see the chief, and the medicine man waiting to greet him. Several braves in full headdresses stood behind them.

Yaweta decided he would be wise to demonstrate his might and the efficiency of the sword. A small tree, a little less than the width of his palm in diameter, grew beside the trail. Trying to show as little effort as possible, he cut it down with a swing of the sword. He could see the surprise on the faces near him, but no sound was made. He cut off a small branch with his knife and found a section, with no knots, about as long as his finger. He slipped the bark away from the end of the piece without cutting it and carved a whistle. Sojata blew on the whistle a few times, and then handed it to a small boy. The boy grabbed it and started blowing in short bursts and doing a dance. The two travelers laughed at his antics.

As they approached the chief Yaweta gave the sign of peace. The sign was returned and they were invited to sit by the fire. Sojata understood some of the language and helped interpret. With this, and sign language, they communicated. The chief told about his tribe and the tribes of his nation. He bragged about the exploits of the braves in war, being sure to impress upon Yaweta how brave they were. Then he began to relate the story of the battle with the giant and his strange weapon.

Sojata affirmed the story told by the raiding party and spent some time bragging about the battle on behalf of Yaweta. He explained that Yaweta never talked about his exploits as is the manner of most braves. Sojata gave the impression that the strange warrior with the strange weapons was some type of mystic being who could not be killed. Yaweta had to spend some time assuring the chief of his peaceful intentions. When Sojata told the name Sean had been given the chief and all the people seemed relieved. That evening Yaweta and Sojata were honored by a feast. The braves Yaweta defeated in battle told about the battle as though it were a great honor to have been defeated and a privilege to have been there.

Now that the stories told by the raiding party were proven to be true, the story spread. Yaweta became known to every tribe in and around the Great Plains. From the mountains to the west to the big river in the east and from the land of constant snow to the desert lands in the south, Yaweta and Sojata were known. Most native tribes had a name that meant something akin to "The People". When "Yaweta" was translated into the local language "Giant Protector of the People" invariably meant the "Giant Protector" of that particular tribe. Therefore he was not looked upon as an enemy but rather as a friend. Many tribes, never having seen him, thought of him as a god rather than a human.

They were given a tepee, next to that of the chief, in which to spend the night. When they came out the next morning a great pile of gifts had been brought by the members of the tribe and left at the door. The chief was standing there waiting. Yaweta refused the gifts but knew his refusal might be insulting to his friends. He explained about the journey they were making and that they could not take so many things with them. When the chief understood their decision to go along the river to its end he waved a brave over and spoke to him in low tones. The two explorers were led over to the river's bank and presented with the chief's canoe and provisions for the trail.

They were told about the trail as far as where this river emptied into an even bigger one. The chief had heard tales of the great waters where the bigger river ended but had never been that far south. Yaweta and Sojata bid their new friends goodbye and left. Their travels were much easier and faster in the canoe. A month later they arrived at a very big river. It flowed nearly straight south.

3.
THE BIG RIVER

Another village was situated at the junction of the two rivers. As they approached they saw the banks lined with natives. They were greeted with awe and wonder. When asked why they chose to honor them with a visit Yaweta told the chief and elders of the tribe that he was there to help them. They stayed with these people over a week.

In the early hours one morning they were hit by a large raiding party from a tribe to the west. When Yaweta came out of the tepee he was using, sword in hand, and began to fight complete chaos erupted. He waded into the main body of the raiders, slashing left and right. Sojata stood at his back to protect the flank. The raiding natives were taken completely by surprise. They ran in fear of the giant white warrior. A few fell victim to the sword. Yaweta had saved the village. His claim of having come to help them had come true. The next day the travelers moved on and their reputation grew to even greater proportions.

Whenever they visited a village they brought something with them as a gift. Generally it was meat. Yaweta would kill an animal and bring it to the central fire. It was easy for him to bag one of the shaggy beasts of the plain. When he carried a six to eight hundred pound Buffalo over his shoulders into the camp and dumped it in front of the fire, it served two purposes. It gave the tribe food and demonstrated his strength. Seldom did he have any trouble.

At one village he was challenged to a wrestling match. A large brave, the biggest he had ever seen, stood before him. The man was nearly as tall as he was and weighed almost as much. With whoops of joy the Indians formed a circle. They faced each other, bare to the waist, and circled around waiting for an opening. The brave, who was called "Mighty Man", saw an opening and lunged. Yaweta's mind went back to the days when he was Sean in the streets of Dublin. He stepped aside and let the native rush past him. As Mighty Man went by Yaweta placed a hand on his back and shoved. Mighty Man hit the dirt. As he started to rise Yaweta pushed him down again with a foot to his rear. He rolled and sprang to his feet just a little peeved. Yaweta knew he was in some trouble. Mighty Man lunged again. As Yaweta dodged Mighty Man changed direction and caught him around the hips. With a mighty heave he lifted Yaweta's feet from the ground. Yaweta was thrown toward the ground but he hit rolling and had hardly touched it when he was on his feet again. Mighty Man had not fully recovered from his effort. Yaweta hoisted him above his head then stepped back and let Mighty Man fall to the ground on his back. When Mighty Man caught him again Yaweta went completely limp. Mighty Man was pulled to the ground by the dead weight of Yaweta. As they hit the ground Yaweta rolled over, winding up sitting on Mighty Man's chest, his knees on the Indian's arms. Yaweta raised his arms and gave a victory yell. After helping Mighty Man up he thanked him for a good fight. The two big men became good friends.

As fall approached they were far down the big river. Leaves were turning yellow when they decided to stop. They picked a spot where they could be alone. Yaweta and Sojata pitched their tepee in a wooded area beside the great river. With fresh water handy, plenty of game, and comfortable quarters, they settled in to wait for the deep snows. It was two months before they saw snow. The weather remained cool but no snow was on the ground. It rained often. When the white flakes finally fell it was not over ankle deep.

Yaweta had lost all track of dates but he knew this was his fourth winter in the new land. His education in the ways of Indians was complete and he was well known in the land. He had inquired of the different tribes about his companions, but no one had any information. There were rumors of a tribe to the far north that had some white warriors but they did not live near any coast so Yaweta did not think they could be his people. The land was a lot larger than they had first figured but he still felt the southern coast could not be much farther. When the first snow melted in just a few days and the weather got better they knew it would be a very mild winter. It snowed off and on but never deep. The days and nights were cold but not like farther north.

Although they thought they had picked a spot far from any village they had visitors. A chief, medicine man, and war chief appeared at the camp one evening with a gift of a deer. They cooked a hindquarter and had a feast while visiting. A mountain lion had killed a child from their village. They wanted the Giant Protector of the People to help. Since they believed the spirits of their greatest chiefs were in the animal, the natives felt they had offended some god. Mountain lions were not known to kill humans. Even the elders of the tribe had never heard of such an event. Sojata stood, solemnly, and promised Yaweta's help as though it were a special gift. The young man enjoyed his role as the son of a god, and played it well.

After three days of hunting they spotted their game among some rocks. The animal was old and could no longer survive in the normal manner of mountain lions so had killed the easier prey of a small child to survive. Yaweta left the others and crept up on the animal. When he felt he was close enough he put an arrow to the string and raised his bow. The arrow flew straight and true nearly twice as far as a native bow could send an arrow. It hit its mark and the animal was dead. Yaweta returned to his tepee without participating in the celebration that followed. A few days later he was presented with a lion fur jacket. It was the fur of the animal he had killed and it fit over his armor. He only wore the armor when he was around others or suspected he may need it. As a rule he wore the buckskins of the northern tribes, or nothing more than a breechcloth as any other Indian would dress.

Hard rains came and stayed for days as the big river got even bigger. When they awoke on the third day, their camp, which had been away from the water's edge a good distance, was on the shoreline and the water was rising. They broke camp and loaded the canoe. Within an hour the campsite was under water. They rowed down river and to higher ground. The river had risen to cover the lower plain. What had been a large river big enough for oceangoing ships of the day had become a vast lake. Except for the strong current and debris in the main channel they could not tell where the river and the normal banks were supposed to be. There was little need to paddle since the canoe was propelled by the current. The explorers were carried rapidly downstream on the floodwaters. Their only concern was the vicious snags under the water. Even when the flood receded the river was very wide and the current strong when they got too far from the bank. The water was dark with mud and very deep.

In a few days another big river joined the one they were traveling. It too had been flooded. The water was equally muddy and whole trees floated in the main current. A little farther downstream, a gigantic logjam blocked all but the middle of the river. They paddled toward the opening, but common sense told them it would be much better to carry their boat around and launch it on the downriver side of the jam. The brush was very thick and still flooded. The men had to wade in water chest deep and cut their way through. Cutting the brush far enough under the water to allow the canoe to pass was difficult and tedious, so the going was slow.

Being smaller, Sojata was swimming as often as walking. The footing was treacherous and they stumbled frequently. About halfway through Sojata sprained his ankle. He never said a word about in until they were back in the river. As he climbed into the canoe Yaweta saw him wince with pain. His ankle was swollen to the same size as his calf. They sought dry land at the first opportunity and made camp. Yaweta carried Sojata to a place beside the fire and put him down. He wet some leather and wrapped the ankle. As the leather dried it served as an effective brace. Several days passed before he would allow his son to try walking. A day or two later he felt the boy could travel. Another week would pass before he would remove the brace.

The day they left the camp they were nearly sunk by trees. The logjam upstream had finally given way and was coming down the river. The canoe was a little way from the main current and moving at a steady pace when Sojata looked back and saw the wall of flotsam coming behind them. They started paddling as fast as possible toward a small island. The logs were catching them as they passed the island and swung in behind it. The flotilla was split by the island. Tree branches reached for them as they floated by the canoe, some within inches. They paddled the canoe to the shore of the island and pulled it onto a little grass beach. They were safe but stuck on the island the rest of the day. The heavy flood of debris from the logjam made it too dangerous to go back into the river.

The small island was actually the top of a hill at the end of a peninsula. The high water had made it an island and had trapped a bear. The bear had not eaten in several days and saw the two humans as a good meal. He was not so starved that his instincts did not recognize danger in Yaweta's sword. The man and the beast stalked each other several minutes as each looked the other over. Sojata pulled a large chunk of deer meat from the canoe and tossed it toward the bear. The bear took the meat. A few more chunks and the bear's hunger was satisfied. The animal and the humans guardedly tolerated each other through the night. In the morning the danger was over and the travelers left, leaving behind the rest of their fresh meat for the bear. In another day or two the water would be low enough for the animal to leave.

The river began to twist and turn its way through a range of hills. At a place where a fair-sized river entered, a native village was established. They saw smoke from the village early in the day so Yaweta dressed in his armor. They decided to stop for a few days when the tribe did not appear to be hostile. A hunting party had seen the canoe just after Yaweta got into his armor so the tribe had gathered and was watching the big white warrior and his son as they came down the river.

The natives had heard of this man but were skeptical about his power. As a demonstration, Yaweta consented to stand in front of five of the best marksmen in the tribe. A red spot was placed in the center of his chest. Yaweta was wearing the lion-fur jacket over his armor. Each native fired one arrow at the target and either hit the mark or very close to it. Three arrows bounced off the armor, and two hung up in the fur of the jacket.

Yaweta pulled the two arrows loose and broke them in half.

Then he took his longbow from his shoulder and fitted an arrow to the string. Two of the braves stood forward and volunteered to take his arrow as he had taken theirs. Yaweta motioned for the two natives to come to him. He sent Sojata off to stand by a tree some distance away and told the two braves to shoot at him. They tried but their arrows fell short about three fourths of the way. Yaweta then shot directly at his son. Sojata sidestepped and caught the arrow as it sailed past. He brought the arrow back and handed it to his father. It was a trick they had practiced many times.

They hunted and fished with the natives for several days. During the first fishing expedition one of the braves speared a fish with a large head and whiskers. It was as ugly as any fish either of the travelers had ever seen. When it was prepared and served it didn't taste nearly as bad as it looked.

Weeks later they came to a place where the river flowed through a vast swamp with small islands here and there. Shortly after entering the swamp they were introduced to some of the wildlife. They had gotten off the main channel and into the swamp. A snake was swimming toward the canoe. Yaweta had seen snakes but never one like this. It was as big around as a man's head, and longer than the big canoe. He never liked snakes and this one was no exception. As the reptile approached the canoe its head was out of the water. Yaweta severed the head with a swipe of the sword. The rest of the body thrashed the water.

Three "logs" came to life and swam toward the canoe. Gigantic mouths opened and a feeding frenzy over the carcass of the snake commenced. The men backed the canoe away and watched. They learned to recognize the difference between real logs and this variety. Yaweta considered the alligator an overgrown, swimming lizard and very dangerous. Although careful, they were nearly capsized by the big lizards three different times.

There were almost constant rains, sometimes heavy but generally just a steady, light rain. In the mornings it was usually foggy, with an eerie mist hanging over the swamp. The trees were covered with moss. Long strands of the green fungus hung down from the branches in the constantly defused light. With the heat, humidity, and constant fight with insects to keep from being eaten alive, the two men were anxious to leave this depressing area. They went back to, and stayed with the main current of the river. At night they would camp on one of the islands, after driving away the crocodiles and the snakes. They cleared a large area and built a circular fire around it for protection. They slept in the middle, surrounded by the fire and hot coals. When they finally found the mouth of the river and salt water they were greatly relieved.

4.
HURRICANE

Sure they had found the south shore of the land; they turned west and attempted to navigate the small craft in the ocean waves. They were driven back to the shoreline. The swamps were still there for another six weeks as they paddled in and out of many inlets and around islands.

Eventually the swamps ended and the shoreline was more defined. Twice they headed north, each time wondering if they had reached the west coast so soon. Once for a whole day, and once for two full days, only to discover they were in a large bay.

At the north end of the second bay they decided to spend some time and rest for a while. The weather had finally gotten cold, and winter was there. Game was plentiful but the deer were small in comparison to the ones in the north. Cold rain fell frequently but no snow. One evening they went into their tepee with a steady cold rain falling. During the night the temperature dropped and when they came out the next morning everything was covered with a layer of ice. The cold weather lasted and the ice did not leave for three days.

The tribes in the area were somewhat hostile, not wanting to trade or talk with them. Yaweta made his usual attempt to meet with the chief. His overtures were rejected. He was told to take his food gift and leave their territory. Not wishing to remain where they were not wanted they prepared to leave only to discover that the canoe had a rip in it. A sharp stone had ripped it when Sojata had pulled it onto the beach.

They found suitable bark and began to make repairs but it was too late. During the night a war party came. Yaweta and Sojata could hear their signals as they got into position for an early morning attack. With their backs to the water of the bay and the enemy on three sides their camp was surrounded.

Yaweta slipped out of the tepee during the dark of the moon. Sojata went out in the opposite direction. When daylight came the attack was launched. The entire party of twelve braves converged on the tepee only to find it empty. Sojata fired arrows into their midst, killing two of them. The raiders took up a defensive position behind a fallen tree. Yaweta walked toward them in full view. Arrows bounced from his armor as his sword slashed out, knocking others out of the air. As they stood staring in amazement all their attention was directed at Yaweta. Sojata charged. At the same time Yaweta charged with a great yell swinging his sword. The natives were suddenly disorganized and confused. Instead of being the attackers they were being attacked. One enemy they wished to destroy would not fall when arrows struck him. The other one simply ducked and avoided their missiles.

The two explorers hit with a vengeance. Sojata killed two more with his knife. Yaweta's sword dispatched the rest. When it was over only the leader of the war party was alive but was bleeding badly. Sojata bound the man's wounds while Yaweta talked to him in sign language. He sent the brave back to his people to tell the story of what had happened and give a warning. Since they had rejected him when he came in peace he would leave them alone. The tribe would never have the protection of the Giant Protector of the People. The day would come, when they would lose their homeland forever. They would be forced to live in the swamps. The warrior who could not be killed had spoken. There would be no reprieve. If they attempted to attack again, the warrior who could not be killed with arrows would destroy all of them.

The next day the repairs were completed on the canoe so the two men left immediately. Yaweta did not want the tribe to test his ability to enforce his prediction. A low fog had settled over the water and the canoe quickly disappeared into the mist. By the time another, much larger, war party appeared there was no sign of the camp. Yaweta's prophecy was repeated in their campfires. It became part of their lore.

After getting out of the bay the men discovered that there was a string of long, narrow islands along the coast. It was much easier to navigate between the islands and the coastline so they made good time. They camped late and left early until they were well away from that tribe of natives. Eventually, they came to a dead end. Land reached from the island on their left to the mainland on their right. They camped for the night. It was a short portage to the other side so they carried the canoe over the following morning.

They had been traveling in a southwest direction; now the shoreline was almost directly north and south. Again they wondered if they would be going up the western coast. They traveled a full day and camped. They next day, about the middle of the afternoon, they found they were heading southeast. It was another large bay. They went in, and out of, large bays three more times. Eventually they found themselves rowing straight south. It was then the hurricane hit.

The sky turned dark and it started to rain hard. There was so much water the canoe was in danger of filling. The wind started to blow. Even in the sheltered area between the island and the shore the water became very choppy. They pulled into a small cove to wait out the storm, pulling the canoe well up on the shore by some big rocks. The rocks formed an overhang that gave a little protection from the weather. The wind became stronger, blowing straight off the water from the southeast and into their shelter. They could see the long low island they had been using for protection to avoid the ocean waves. A great wall of water washed over the island, completely covering it. Trees were uprooted by the force of water and wind. They rode the waves like pieces of bark. The island broke the main force but still a smaller wave came up and drenched the men. As the water started receding the canoe started to go with it. In desperation they pulled it back and put it in the overhang behind them just in time to avoid a tree falling where the canoe had been only seconds before.

Wave after wave buffeted the shore until the men felt they would drown if they stayed where they were. Yaweta went out and pulled the fallen tree close to the opening of the shelter so the branches covered the entrance. Sojata piled loose rocks in the canoe to hold it down. It had only been an hour or more since the rain first started, but it seemed like a day. The men traveled straight inland, away from the water. They had gone over a mile before they went over a little hill and found another overhang. This one was facing away from the wind and rain. Dry wood and leaves were in the shelter so they built a fire to dry out and warm themselves.

Once a good fire was started, they could use some of the wet wood from outside their shelter to keep it going. The wind was not so strong on this side of the hill but the rain kept up its downpour. They could hear the storm even after it was too dark to see. It was a long, cold night. By dawn the storm had passed over them. In the morning sky they could see the storm marching across the land in the clouds and the stream of rain coming down from them. Sojata spied a deer. He got as close as

39

possible and killed it with an arrow. They carried the meat to the place where they had left the canoe.

Along the shoreline was devastation. Numerous trees were uprooted, and big boulders had been moved by the waves. The canoe had been saved by a miracle. Trees had been washed up in front of the overhang, blocking it and keeping the canoe inside. The rocks prevented it from bouncing around and breaking apart. After removing the trees they found the canoe completely filled with water. A good-sized sea bass was swimming in it. All of their food was ruined by the saltwater. The deer meat and the fish were their only provisions. They built a fire; dried their belongings, made a few repairs, and got reorganized. Two days later they continued on their way under a bright sun.

5.
TORNADO

Eventually, the two explorers camped for a week at the mouth of a good-sized river that came from the west. The chain of islands seemed to direct their travels right into the mouth of the river. While there, they took another look at their progress, and mission. This land was obviously a lot larger than Captain Mac had assumed, or anyone had even dreamed. Yaweta decided he wanted to follow the river toward the west. This route would probably be faster to the west coast and closer to the camp of the ship's crew. Yaweta longed for their company. Neither man had any desire to spend any more time on this coast. A month later they were far up the river and away from the ocean.

By now Sojata was a young man. He was tall, slim and quick. There was more strength in his long, stringy, frame than it appeared. He had earned the title of brave by killing his enemies in battle, and Yaweta was proud to call him his son. He had learned Yaweta's strange language very quickly and was a good companion.

Yaweta looked and acted more Indian than European. His skin had darkened in the hot sun, and he had taken on all the mannerisms of an Indian brave. Two things betrayed his heritage - his blue eyes and his auburn hair. He had a full beard, and the hair on his chest, arms, and legs was particularly thick. Sojata teased him about being part bear.

Birch-bark canoes, by their nature, suffer a little wear so they camped to make repairs and to replenish their supply of food. Their main diet, when they could not find fresh meat, was the dried trail meat Yaweta had learned to make when he first started. They were camped just up a small stream off the river. It was a wooded area with plenty of game, large clear areas to the east and west, and only a thin line of trees following the creek north. A better defensive position could not be found. Danger did not come from marauding Indians. It came from nature in the middle of a hot, muggy day.

During the time when animals usually find shade in which to rest Yaweta saw the animals of the area migrating in a hurried manner to the west. There was every kind of animal, grass feeders as well as predators, traveling without any fear of one another. It was almost as if a fire were driving them. The men became concerned. If a fire was coming they would be better off in the river so they began to break camp. They could not smell smoke but the animals definitely were running from something.

What was a bright sunny day suddenly turned dark. The sky filled with clouds. Lightning danced in the sky and the wind increased. It looked as though it would rain and extinguish any fire the animals were trying to escape. The men relaxed a little, but continued to break camp figuring to go on upriver.

The sky turned a greenish color. In the distance they could see clouds form a funnel shape and dip toward the earth. To the southeast one of the funnel shaped clouds was coming straight toward their campsite. Yaweta saw trees being ripped out of the ground and taken up into the funnel. A defining roar filled the air. He yelled at Sojata to follow him. Upstream a short distance was a washout ditch formed by rainwater drainage to the stream. This small shelter was the only place to hide from the funnel so they sought its meager protection. The ditch was fairly deep and narrow, but long enough for both men to lie down. They dove into the mud and water and lay there afraid to move as the wind blew above them but the funnel never found them.

The adventurers watched as the funnel came toward them. They saw it reach the camp a few strides away. Their entire camp was taken up and disappeared into the funnel. Whole trees, roots and all were taken. They ducked down and waited for the wind to reach them. After a few minutes Yaweta raised his head. Rain had started to fall but the darker storm clouds were traveling out of the area toward the north. They stood and watched the progress of the storm for several moments before they took stock of their situation. The tornado had devastated camp, but in just the short distance between the campsite and where they were hiding it had lifted. The trees were untouched for a distance, and then the funnel touched earth again. It was as though a giant had walked along, leaving footprints of devastation across the landscape.

The canoe was missing, as was everything they did not have with them in the washout. There seemed to be nothing else to do but to track the tornado and see if they could find any of their belongings. Yaweta felt he would need his armor, and his sword was missing. He thought he had grabbed it when he ran for the ditch but it must have dropped from his grasp in the rush. The sun came from behind the clouds and the rain stopped. The day was as it was before the storm. Not far away they saw the reflection of something metal. It was Yaweta's breastplate. Parts and pieces of Yaweta's armor were scattered about and the men found each part as they searched the rest of the day. Various items were found, an article of clothing here, a buffalo robe there, but the big sword was nowhere in sight. There was a strange and complete absence of any part of the canoe.

It was interesting to see the strange things the storm had done. An entire tree had been pulled up, roots and all, and turned over. The tree was then jammed back into the ground so the branches were down and the roots up, as though it were standing on its head. They saw grass in the side of trees as though it grew there. A small tree had been broken off and was sticking through a bigger tree, one end on each side. Yaweta could have sworn a hole had been drilled in the big tree and the small tree inserted.   When they found his helmet it was sitting on the stump of a small tree that had been broken off about head high to Sojata. Sojata thought it funny that the stump was wearing the helmet.

They had traveled half a day when they saw something shining on the face of sandstone outcropping at the edge of one of the tornado's footprints. The cliff was at least three times as high as Yaweta so it was unusual in this more or less flat country. As they approached to investigate they were astounded to discover the sword imbedded in the rock. It was lying flat against the face of the cliff as though the rock had formed around it. Sojata stood on Yaweta's shoulders and reached up to pry it loose with his knife. It came down and stuck into the ground at Yaweta's feet. The perfect outline of the sword remained in the rock. The sword had taken quite a beating. Yaweta sharpened it on sandstone and replaced it in his scabbard.

The trail of the wind finally quit. The funnel had returned to the sky from which it came. As they traveled they came across a small lake in a depression, with no inlet or outlet as with other lakes. This seemed to be strictly a rainwater lake. Floating in the shallow lake was the canoe. Yaweta waded out and pulled it to shore. The canoe had a little water in it, but was intact, almost without a scratch. Yaweta knew Captain Mac would never believe the strange behavior of the tornado. It would be a subject for good-natured debate and jibes for a long time.

They decided to take the canoe back to the river. Two days later they arrived. They camped for a week to rest, prepare some more jerky for the trail, and make a new paddle for their canoe. The paddle was constructed from a branch with a fork in it. The two branches of the fork were bent around and tied. Then the resulting tear-shaped end was covered with a solid leather piece sewn over it. With new food and the salvaged items, they were ready to continue on their journey. The river became more and more difficult to travel with frequent rapids and portages.

They were camped after carrying the canoe around one of the rough-water areas. During the night Sojata, who was sleeping near the canoe, was awakened by a noise. A bear was at the canoe. It evidently smelled the meat or fish that had been carried in it. The bear pushed the canoe over and mauled it, breaking the bottom. Eventually it pushed the canoe into the rapids with a grunt. Sojata started yelling at the bear when he fist saw it. Yaweta joined in the effort to scare the bear away. The bear lumbered off but not before the canoe was lost. They did not consider building another one. Since the river was becoming smaller and there were so many portages they decided to travel by foot.

A trail beside the river was leading in a northwesterly direction, away from the river. They suspected that land away from this source of water would arid, as they had discovered in their trek to get back to the river earlier. They took along water bags made from animal stomachs. Each one, when dried, would hold enough water to last several days. Carrying two water bags each, and a supply of dried meat, they started up the trail.

The river had started west then took them northwest. When they left the river it was flowing from the north. To the west of the river was a range of mountains. It looked as though the trail would take them into those hills. The mountains were not like the ones in the north with trees and streams. These were barren and without water. It would be a desolate place.

6.
ENEMY

Two days later Yaweta suddenly stopped and slipped behind a rock to put on his armor. He had seen an Indian some distance away, crossing a low hill. The men did not try to avoid contact with the natives. They rather looked forward to learning something about the trail ahead. Farther along there were several braves waiting to greet them on the trail. They seemed friendly and were very curious about the big white warrior and his weapons. They guided the explorers to an encampment of some forty or fifty braves. Most of them were wearing war paint so it was obvious they were a war party. The War Chief greeted them as they approached the camp. Meat was cooking on the fire and the meal was ready.

After eating the explorers were invited to speak. Sojata went into his usual exaggerated account of their exploits. He made Yaweta almost a god and said he was the son. Sign language was their only means of communication because of the different languages, but was very effective. At the end of the speech, when he gave Yaweta's name there was a murmuring in the crowd.

While Sojata spoke the War Chief stood on the opposite side of the fire. Now the War Chief spoke and it was Sojata's turn to stand opposite and listen. The Chief bragged at long length of the tribe's bravery and victories over every other tribe. He pointed to the north, east, south, and west calling all but his tribe weaklings and in need of a champion to do their battles for them. The name of his tribe could only mean "Enemy". They were the Indians later called, "Apache". His speech was directed toward Sojata because he was the one to speak, just as Sojata had spoken to him.

The other members of the tribe were spectators listening to a conversation as was the custom. Yaweta sat in the front of the circle next to where the War Chief had been sitting when the speeches began. Sojata's seat was on the other side of the War Chief's place. Their weapons lay on the ground beside their seating places. The Chief motioned for another brave, obviously the second in command to speak and sat down. Sojata sat down to listen.

The brave began speaking by bragging about his bravery in a recent battle then talked of how poorly the enemy fought. Then his motions indicated that this tribe had no need of a protector of the people and the idea that they would need help was an insult. He quit signing and shouted words in his own tongue working the crowd to a frenzy.

Both Yaweta and Sojata reached for their weapons as they saw what was happening but it was too late. Loops of leather were thrown over them. Although they fought hard they were overcome by the mass of bodies. After a terrific struggle Yaweta was laying on his back spread out with hands and feet tied to stakes in the ground. He lifted his head and saw Sojata some distance away in a similar predicament.

The War Chief had Yaweta's sword. It was too heavy for him. He did not know how to handle the unfamiliar weapon, so he had trouble controlling it. He wounded two of his own braves before trying to cut a tree. It was a strong swing. The blade sank into the tree as deep as the width of the blade itself and stayed there. He tried to pull the blade straight out, but it was stuck. Not wanting to show his ignorance, or lack of strength, he left the sword as though he had meant to leave it stuck in the tree.

Six braves guarded Yaweta. One of them saw him looking around and poked him with a spear. The spear hit the breastplate under Yaweta's jacket with a metallic sound. The native must have thought it strange when Yaweta didn't flinch but didn't have time to inquire. Two of the other braves put a leather band over Yaweta's head and staked it down so he could not move his head. Then something at the fire got their attention. Yaweta could hear a celebration going on but could not see what was happening or understand their language. He lay there wondering what was going to happen to them and hoping Sojata was safe.

Sojata was first to experience the Indian's idea of sport. A strong belief, held by natives of all tribes, in being able to withstand pain without crying out kept Sojata from screaming as they tortured him. At first they laughed when they kicked him and stuck him with spears as he lay staked out on the ground. When he did not make a sound the play got rougher. His fingers and toes were broken one by one, then his arms and legs. Perspiration poured from his forehead. Tears ran out of his eyes and his teeth were clamped tightly but Sojata never made a sound. His body convulsed as nerves reacted with muscles. The braves were overjoyed to find such a worthy brave.

This was obviously a brave with much power and when he finally died they would acquire that power from the dead man. The more torture he could endure, the more power he had, and the more they would receive. As they tortured him they chanted compliments and sang praises to him. In their twisted way he had become somewhat of a hero so they prolonged his death to honor him.

Sojata knew he would eventually die and had no intention of entering the afterlife in disgrace. He would

49

be honored by the Great Spirit, and even Yaweta's God. Yaweta had told him of the God of the white men. To Sojata this God seemed to be the Great Spirit by another name, or they could be brothers. Sojata concentrated on this and his own tribe's concept of life after death. It helped him endure the pain.

His tormenters began to rip large portions of skin from his body. They cut a flap away then grasped it and pulled until a strip came loose then danced around with it. When they tired of that they started cutting away parts of his body. Whenever he passed out they would throw water on him. Eventually consciousness would return. The torture continued for two days. Just as the Great Spirit, blood brother of God, gathered Sojata into his arms, the young brave called out to his father in a loud voice, "Yaweta".

When Yaweta heard his son's voice his head automatically raised pulling the pegs holding the strap across his head out of the ground. Yaweta saw what they had been doing to Sojata. The youth was to be the preliminary entertainment. Yaweta was to be the main attraction. His death was to be a lot slower and more painful. Blind rage took over Yaweta at the sight of his son's mutilated body.

The big Irishman, turned Indian, was normally a powerful man with extraordinary strength. Adrenalin made him ten times as strong. Rage made him act. Usually the Irish have a quick temper, but get over it just as fast. This Irishman was different. His rage was born in the death of his parents at the hands of rapists and murderers and was nourished by the death of his son.

His hands twisted around and grasped the pegs to which they were tied and pulled them out of the ground. When the pegs holding his legs down came loose he never even noticed. In half a minute he was loose and had killed two of his guards by driving the pegs in his hands into them. One of the pegs broke, freeing his left hand. As he used the peg in his right hand to dispatch another, grabbing the man's stone knife with his left. He threw the knife into the throat of another of his guards. As he yanked the peg out of the chest of the one, it broke, freeing his right hand completely. The last two guards charged in. Ignoring their weapons, he grabbed one with each hand and crashed their heads together. Their heads cracked like eggs falling on rocks.

His rage did not make him dumb. Yaweta ran to his sword. With one hand he pushed against the tree while pulling the sword away from the cut. Now that he had his sword he cut the leather straps around his ankles and wrists. With a sound that echoed through the rocks and canyons of the mountains he charged the main body of the war party.

The adrenalin flowed in his veins and all the rage of his life was in him. His sword never slowed it's ark as he waded into them. As they swarmed around him his sword took its toll. His left arm brushed away those who jumped on him as though they were flies. His voice, still ringing, mingled with the screams of the dying and the sound of steel on flesh and bone. The Indians broke and ran. Yaweta chased after them, the blade still cutting them down like a farmer's scythe cutting grain. Six of the warriors escaped the initial onslaught but were bleeding. The avenging Yaweta followed their trail of blood. One bled to death and lay on the trail. The other five were struggling up a steep hill when Yaweta caught them. The battle took only seconds and the hunt for the six less than a half hour.

Yaweta felt the aftermath of the battle as he returned to find his son. His body shook as the adrenalin left it and sorrow took over. Yaweta picked up the body of his son and carried it to a high place. The sound of his sorrow went over the land throughout the night. In the morning he buried the lad and built a monument of rocks to mark his resting place and honor his memory.

He stacked the bodies of the braves who died that night in a huge pile, stripping them so they would enter the next life naked and ashamed. While taking their clothing he found the steel knives the natives had stolen from him and Sojata. His bow was on the body of the War Chief. He hacked this body into small pieces and scattered them to the four winds.

He took a part of the body to make a pouch. This native would never enter the afterlife and would have no power. He would wander forever in limbo looking for his missing part. This was the belief of the natives, and Yaweta hoped it was true. He took everything he wanted from the camp and destroyed the rest, burning what he could and being sure to break every weapon. They believed their weapons accompanied them to the next life. These would have no weapons if the belief was true.

Yaweta, the Indian, did these things to shame his enemies. Sean, the Irishman, did these things to warn others. He knew some of the tribe would come to investigate the smoke from the fire. There were enough signs to show that one man had done this. Whoever came would be able to read the story in the signs. He left the bodies to feed the scavengers of the air and the land. The tribe called Enemy had found one.

Yaweta did not get away without being hurt. Numerous stab wounds and cuts bled on his arms and legs. Eventually they took their toll. The great strength he had during the battle became a great weakness. He bathed in the water and ate some of the meat left over from the night before. As weak as he felt he wanted to leave this place so he traveled west away from the trail. Late in the day he lay down in a small cave to rest. He passed out from exhaustion and loss of blood. When he awoke a wet piece of leather was being applied to his wounds.

The Giant Protector of the People had been found by some boys from the Cliff Dwellers tribe. They had been out on a trial of manhood when they came across the white warrior and summoned help. It took eight men a full day to carry Yaweta across the mountains to their dwelling. Yaweta lay still, looking around. At first he thought he was in a cave but soon realized it was a house. It was the first house he had seen since he left Erin. His wounds were bound and a young girl of about sixteen sat by his side, ministering to his needs. When she felt his eyes on her she called out.

7.
CLIFF DWELLERS

Yaweta did not understand her words but could not help being impressed by the soft musical qualities of her voice. Dressed in soft, beaded doeskin, she stood up and walked to the door calling out again. She was not tall. He figured she would be able to walk under his outstretched arm with ease. He had not seen a woman walk with such grace since he was a young boy. When she turned to walk toward him he saw her face clearly. It was slightly round, and pretty, with an intelligent, yet mischievous look in her brown eyes. Before he could speak to her a man walked in.

A woman and two young men came behind him. The girl left and came back with a bowl of broth. She fed him with a spoon insisting that he lie still. When the broth was finished he smiled his thanks and closed his eyes. Two hours later he woke up fully alert. While sleeping he dreamed.

He was with the girl beside one of the small mountain streams in the north. There was a tepee and fire as though they were living at the place. She came to him dressed all in white and holding her arms out toward him. He folded her in his arms and kissed her. Then he picked her up and carried her over to the tepee. As they entered the tepee the dream faded. He woke up but didn't open his eyes. He wanted to savor the feeling of contentment and peace the dream gave him. When his eyes opened the girl was sitting at his feet watching him with a mystical look in her eyes and a slight smile on her lips.

These Indians were shorter than most he had seen. They were all slightly round faced and most were slightly heavy. Their language was different from any he had heard. This was not the Enemy tribe. He had fallen into friendly hands. He felt strong enough to get out of bed and did in spite of the girl's objections. The evening meal was being served and he was invited to join. After the meal he learned who these people were and how he came to be with them.

The smoke of his fire had attracted the boys. They read the signs and saw the destruction he had caused and followed his trail, being sure to destroy all sign of his passing as they followed. The boys found him within minutes after he had lost consciousness and one went for help. Ten of the men from the tribe went back to carry him and his things to their village. When the boys told what they had found, they had emphasized his size, so plenty of help had arrived.

These natives were called Cliff Dwellers. Their homes were built from mud and grass and located in a large cavern. The cavern was well up the side of a cliff and only one trail led down to the valley below. A spring of water was at the base of the cliff below the dwellings. They used the cavern because it was easy to defend. With only one trail two warriors could stand guard and give warning before anyone could come close. They had lived here for many years, farther back than anyone could remember, and believed they had been in the village since time began.

Their enemy was the Apache and had raided them many times killing the men and taking the women until there were only a hundred and fifty left. Many of the dwellings were empty. Their hatred of the enemy natives was only surpassed by their fear. They were a peaceful tribe, preferring trade to war. For trade goods they made jewelry from a blue-green stone found in the mountains, and pottery from clay. The pottery was shaped and then cooked in ovens they had built from clay. They were agricultural by nature with gardens of plants Yaweta did not recognize. The Apache had whittled down their numbers by ambushing their hunting and trading parties.

At his request two braves were sent to watch the site of his battle with the Enemies. Two days later he got word that more of the tribe were there and had sent a runner to their village to bring back more braves. It was only four days since Yaweta had fought them but he felt strong. He felt he needed to help these people in their fight against the Enemies and wanted to exact farther revenge. That night he slipped away.

He arrived early in the morning and stood on the high place beside his son's grave. The sentinel who had been there died silently when Yaweta slit his throat. They had started pulling the dead from the pile and were preparing them for burial. Clothing and weapons were being brought in to help the dead enter the afterlife with honor. He noticed that someone had started to uncover his son. Since they had not taken his warning seriously he decided to give them another chance to learn.

In the early dawn as the braves were first starting to stir his voice rang out in a savage yell. He ran through the camp slashing with his sword. Many of them died before he disappeared into the morning mist. A number of them tried to follow his trail but lost it. They went back to camp to organize a search. The chief of the tribe split them into groups of eight to ten and sent them out.

Yaweta visited each group in turn. The first group found him standing at the entrance to a small ravine. As they attacked he cut them down. Their yells and the yell of the avenging Yaweta brought other groups but the avenger was gone. They fanned out looking for him but he avoided them. If they had looked they would have found him in a small cave near where the dead men were laying. An hour later he came out and sought out another hunting party. They heard him in the main camp. Sometime later he was heard again on the other side of the camp. Eight times Yaweta's voice was heard. When night fell only sixteen braves returned to camp. Not one brave had seen the man who antagonized them and lived.

When Yaweta charged the camp he had gone through fast. With the confusion and speed no one had gotten a good look at him. They saw a giant with hair all over his body and a gigantic knife in his hand. Yaweta was wearing his armor but he was also wearing his lion-fur jacket over the breastplate. His naturally hairy body was odd to the smooth skinned, hairless natives. Imagination took over. The tribe could not conceive of one man doing all the damage this one had done. Therefore it could not be a human. The debate around the campfire that night did not concern who was harassing them. It was a question of what was harassing them.

The question was never settled. The talk increased their fear. When Yaweta charged through the camp again he found little resistance, only confusion and fear. Several braves fell to his sword in that one pass. The rest of the night he could be heard outside the range of the firelight. The sky was full of dark clouds and a light rain fell so there was no moon.

Sentries were sent out to guard the camp but they were returned dead. The body of each sentry was flung into the firelight by the unseen man. Six different sentries gave their lives before the chief decided to keep the guard close to the campfire. For several hours during the night Yaweta carried the braves he had killed during the day and flung them at the campfire. Eventually all the dead were back at the camp where he wanted them.

Yaweta used a catapult to send the dead into the fire. He bent a sapling over with a leather rope and tied it down. Then he placed the body on its branches and released the rope. When the sapling straightened out it would fling the dead body toward the campfire. He had five different saplings around the camp that were good for this purpose. Once, he had all five saplings loaded and ran from one to the other to create a bombardment into the mist of the natives. No one in the camp rested that night. When the last body was catapulted into the camp Yaweta rested for an hour. An hour before dawn he used the bows and arrows he had collected from the search parties. He would shoot two or three arrows into the camp then move before the returning fire could reach him and shoot again. Time and time again, he repeated this action until all the arrows were used and the sun began to light the sky.

When full light came the chief and seven other braves were still standing. The seven braves formed a defensive circle around their chief. Yaweta calmly walked toward them. Arrows sailed through the air but only three struck him. All three arrows shattered as they hit the breastplate. The natives dropped their bows and started to run in panic. They were caught and cut down calmly and quickly.

One very young and confused brave lay by the fire sick to his stomach. Yaweta lifted him up and sat him on a rock. With sign language and a gentile voice he calmed the boy's fear. When he felt a little better he was told to return to his village and tell all his people what had happened. He was told the same thing would happen to any of the tribe that came to the place. The young brave left at a dead run.

Yaweta made another pile of dead beside the first. He disgraced them in the same manner as he had the first bunch. The damage caused by the effort to bury the dead and clothe them was repaired. The place was once more a place of shame to the tribe and would remain that way forever. He salvaged the best of the bows, all the arrows, and some other weapons to carry back to his new friends.

The young brave, Yaweta had let live, told a wild story when he returned to his village. Not wanting to admit to being so scared he was sick, and having listened to the talk around the fire, he told of a half-native, half-bear, whom was bigger than two men were and indestructible. He claimed the three arrows that had hit Yaweta were his. He elaborated on the story and was believed, because he was the only survivor of the two war parties.

Thus was born a legend of a half-beast, half-man who roamed the mountains. Yaweta's later actions helped the legend. The place, where Yaweta's revenge had taken place, became a holy place of the dead, and was avoided by members of all tribes. These tales were brought to the Cliff Dwellers a few days after Yaweta returned.

When Yaweta left with the captured weapons, he was joined by the two young men who had found him in the cave. He understood the one to be called Rabbit and the bigger one Grey Wolf. They helped carry the spoils. The boys had witnessed the events of the previous day and night from a distance. They had even considered helping the big warrior but could see they would only be in the way. They did help a little. Twice the boys had distracted search groups while Yaweta was busy.

The two young braves asked about the grave on the high knoll. When Yaweta told them about Sojata they promised to see that no one disturbed his rest. As the years went by they spread stories about seeing ghost natives in the area. With the taboo of a holy place of the dead, the ghost stories worked to keep people away for many years.

When they arrived at the cliff dwelling they were greeted with great enthusiasm. Unlike other tribes the feast of welcome was not a brag session. Yaweta gave the facts and expressed his sorrow at having to kill so many. He told the story of his son, from beginning to end, as an explanation of the necessity. All agreed the first war party had to be killed for revenge. The second war party had to be killed to protect the grave of Sojata. The name Sojata became one of great honor in the tribe.

Yaweta decided to stay with this tribe for a time. A long rest might be beneficial to him and he might be able to help the tribe survive the raids of the Apache. He learned the language of the tribe and began to learn their culture. The natives called Enemy were fierce fighters who terrorized the surrounding tribes and roamed over a vast area, bringing destruction wherever they went.

Yaweta could not help but wonder if the mischievous eyed girl, Singing Bird, had anything to do with his decision to stay awhile. He had taken over an empty house nearby, and she helped him get organized. She helped him learn the tongue and understand their culture during her frequent visits. For some reason they seemed to be together a great deal. Time passed quickly when they were together.

Once he was settled he began to get involved in their crafts. Working with the blue-green stones reminded him of his days as an apprentice jeweler. He recognized the stone as turquoise immediately and knew exactly how to use it. He discovered silver ore in the canyon. Two friends helped him as he carried some of it home. He refined the ore and made a ring for Singing Bird. When the tribe saw the ring everyone wanted one.

Yaweta taught the tribe how to extract silver from the ore, and how to work it to make jewelry. For a time they made silver items with hammered designs. Eventually it was time to graduate to finer things. He took a piece of turquoise and showed them how to polish it and to set it in the silver. Before many months they were making a variety of jewelry. The tribe became famous for their ornaments.

Trade flourished. On one of their trading journeys the party was ambushed and killed by Apaches. The next traders who went out had Yaweta following them. When the trading party was attacked Yaweta was there. Ten of the attackers died. The two who were left ran as though a ghost was after them. From then on Yaweta often went into the surrounding mountains, keeping an eye on hunters and traders, or just wandering around. Many times he ran into parties of Apaches. He killed most of them, and the few who escaped spread the man-beast story. Yaweta knew the story and used it to his advantage. Before long, none of the enemy natives would enter the mountains. Most of the tribes moved their villages away. The Cliff Dwellers were safe.

One day he gave one of the steel knives to Singing Bird's father, picked up her blanket, and carried it to his house. Sometime later a son was born. Two years later, when it was time for a name, the chief insisted on his right to name the child. He called the boy, "Sojata", after Yaweta's son, saying it meant, "Great Chief", and named the child his successor. In a long speech at the naming ceremony he claimed this brave would be the salvation of the Cliff Dwellers and would lead them to victory over all their enemies. He meant it to honor Yaweta.

During the ceremony Yaweta presented the medicine pouch of thin leather he had made from a part of the war chief to the new Sojata. By custom the boy was not Yaweta's son. The chief had no son of his own, so the first-born son of his girl child was his. This saddened Yaweta, but the law had to be followed. He returned Singing Bird's blanket to her father, packed his

61

belongings, and left. He carried with him a good supply of raw turquoise, a number of turquoise beads, and jewelry made of silver and turquoise.

8.
THE CANYON

Yaweta knew a longer stay with the Cliff Dwellers would invite disaster. His culture would clash with theirs in a violent way very soon, so he decided to leave on friendly terms. The law of the Cliff Dwellers when his own son was taken was something he could not long forgive. He knew of a stream a short distance away, which flowed toward the west. It was a good sign. He knew that every stream and river eventually flows into a bigger body of water. If this stream didn't wind up in a lake he would find the west coast. He followed it.

He traveled at a leisurely pace, enjoying the solitude. It was the first time he had been completely alone and found it to be pleasant. As big as he was, his easygoing pace took him a long way at the end of a day. After several days he came across a camp. The three natives there were friendly and acted as though they were used to strangers dropping in. An old man and two young boys lived beside a small creek.

Chips of flint were strewn about the camp. A small pile of arrowheads lay on a flat rock. Yaweta could see the places where the Indians did their work. The old man was a maker of arrows and spears. The two boys were his apprentices. The area contained a large amount of flint and the campsite was good. No Indian would bother the maker of arrowheads because it was a highly skilled trade and everyone needed his product. Arrow maker was a highly respected trade.

The old man greeted Yaweta by name. He had heard the stories about the man-beast and recognized Yaweta as the one. Much of the old man's business was with his own tribe, the Apache, but he dealt with other tribes as well. He was the local newspaper when it came to spreading news of events in the various villages. To learn more about the hair-covered white warrior, he invited him to stay for a while.

Since it was late afternoon, Yaweta decided to spend the night. After the meal Yaweta told about himself. The old man did not understand everything and probably did not believe much of what he did understand but was glad when Yaweta decided to stay. The overnight stay extended itself as the two became better acquainted. When the old arrow maker saw the steel arrowheads Yaweta used, he was greatly impressed. He wanted Yaweta to get him some of the stones that made them so Yaweta told him the material was not available anywhere except across the big waters. The old man only understood that he would not be able to make steel arrowheads.

Yaweta was fascinated with the art of arrowhead making and struck a deal with the old arrow maker. The old man would teach him as he taught his apprentices. In exchange Yaweta would show him a new idea that would help him improve his product.

Yaweta learned how to make flint arrowheads. After making several he brought out a piece of turquoise. He made an arrowhead from the stone. Then he showed them how to polish the turquoise. The old native and the two boys were thrilled. After making several and polishing them, the natives had the process learned.

The area around the camp was a place of peace. No brave would attack another in this area, as a rule, but the old man was sure what would happen if Yaweta were there when his tribe came for a supply of ammunition. A large party was due to come any day so he asked Yaweta to leave. Yaweta did not want war any more than the old man did, so he decided it was time to move down the river. He presented the old man with one of his steel arrowheads. In exchange he took several turquoise arrowheads with him and left most of his turquoise rocks with the old man.

A few days later Yaweta sat to rest on a tree of stone. The place was barren except for a number of petrified trees. Long ago, before history began, there had been a forest of living trees. Now the trees were stones. Yaweta wondered what could have caused such a phenomenon. Wood generally decays but these had not. He contemplated on this but knew of no answer so dismissed it from his mind and moved on.

As he followed the river he passed by villages now and again. Most of them were deserted by the time he arrived. The Indians were so afraid of him they would run and hide. From the markings of the tepees and the things they left behind he knew they were Apache. He understood their fear. If they had come back, he would have attacked.

As he progressed down the river he found himself deeper and deeper into a canyon. The farther he went the more fascinating it was. The sides narrowed and several times he found himself wading in the water. He enjoyed the beauty of the canyon so continued in spite of the difficulty. Two days later he met another tribe of Indians.

They had never heard of him in their isolated stronghold but were curious about him. He was invited to the evening meal. The natives welcomed the chance for a celebration and all gathered by the fire. After the meal the chief spoke, using sign language as well as his own tongue, so Yaweta could understand. He bragged at length about the tribe and their prowess then welcomed Yaweta. It was his turn to speak.

Yaweta was suspicious of the similar situation. Everything was too much like the time his son was killed.

When he got up to speak he was not only wearing his armor under the lion fur jacket, the bow was on his shoulder with the quiver of arrows on his back. He held his sword in his hand. A small pine tree stood near the fire. Yaweta stepped over and cut it down with a single blow. This demonstration worked once before and it seemed to work again. Just to get their attention a little more he struck himself on the chest with the edge of the sword. When he was not hurt and no blood showed he definitely had their attention. He never knew whether their intentions were friendly or not in the beginning but they got more sociable.

He spoke for half an hour. He said he was Yaweta. His signs told them what the name meant. He told of his exploits but didn't brag to impress them. The truth was incredible enough. When he was through he sat down, the chief got up again followed by the medicine man, and the most honored brave of the tribe. Each one spent ten minutes talking about how privileged they were to have him visit and pledged their aid in anything he wanted.

As a gesture of friendship Yaweta presented a turquoise arrowhead to the brave, a medallion of silver to the medicine man, and another silver medallion with a turquoise setting to the chief. In return he was given a big canoe and two braves as guides until he exited the canyon.

They started down the river the next day. One brave was at the front of the canoe and the other in the back. Yaweta was in the middle, with the supplies between them. There were rapids but the two experienced braves negotiated them with skill and daring. Yaweta spent his time looking at the rapidly changing scenery.

The canyon became so deep he could not see the top of the cliffs. It was as though the earth had been split open. There were pentacles of multicolored rock in the canyon floor, mixed with trees. At times they made a portage around rapids and falls, other times there was no choice but to take the water route. After the first day Yaweta was more than ready to camp. During the evening meal he became better acquainted with his companions. The two braves said they had traveled the river many times, but not with a passenger, and especially not one so important.

Yaweta slept very lightly. During the night he found himself awake several times. Twice he would have sworn one of the braves had been approaching him. Both times the brave smiled and walked on by when he saw Yaweta looking at him. The brave would be gone a couple minutes and then return and lie down again. Yaweta still wore his armor and would not remove it with these two around. The next morning he took a leather string and tied it around his wrist. He tied the other end around the hilt and guard of his sword. In case of a problem he did not want to lose it in the river.

Yaweta's senses were alert the full day but nothing happened that could be interpreted as an aggressive move. The night passed equally peacefully. Yaweta began to think his intuition had been wrong. The following day the waters were difficult to maneuver and Yaweta's guard was down. In a particularly rough set of rapids he felt the canoe would capsize several times. Toward the end of the day they were going over some rough water when he felt something hit his back very hard.

The blow was hard enough to bend the back plate of his armor and cause a nasty bruise. The back plate was thinner than the front but the stone tomahawks of the braves were no match for it. Yaweta turned to see the native behind him holding a broken stone tomahawk in disbelief. The big white native's natural and immediate reaction was to backhand the startled native off the canoe and into the water but the sword was in his right hand so he hit the man with the flat side of the weapon. Unfortunately when the native was dumped the canoe rolled over and everyone went into the water.

The two natives floated down the rapids and swam to shore. Yaweta's armor caused him to sink like a rock and roll on the bottom in the swift current. He quickly got rid of his jacket, losing his bow and arrows in the process. His lungs felt as though they would burst as he reached for his knife and cut away the leather that held the two plates of armor together at each side. The thick leather across his shoulders was next. As soon as the armor was gone he was able to reach the surface, gasping for breath. He fought to keep afloat and worked his way toward land, reaching the bank of the river some two hundred yards from the Indians and on the opposite shore.

He rested from his ordeal for a few minutes then took stock of what he had left. His knife was in his left hand and his sword was still hanging from his wrist. The leather string had cut his wrist as the sword dragged along the bottom of the river. The blade was pretty beat up and the leather string had almost broken. He cut the string away and soaked the wound to ease the pain. He was naked to the waist and had the knife, sword, breeches, and a turquoise and silver medallion around his neck. About a dozen turquoise arrowheads were in the pocket of his breeches. He felt fortunate to be so well armed and alive. After a while he started downstream.

He was almost out of the canyon and the going was easier. After a couple hours he was lucky enough to kill a rabbit for food by throwing his knife. He started a fire with two sticks and roasted the meat. He felt a lot better after a good meal and a night's rest. The next day he found pieces of the canoe and the paddle floating in the water but none of the gear that had been in the boat.

He traveled the river for two weeks. In that time he improved his lot. He built another bow and strung it with leather strips he cut from his leggings. He made arrow shafts from willow branches and tied turquoise arrowheads on with sinew from the rabbit. He found a bird feather here and there and used them for stabilizing feathers. Before long he killed a deer. He made a backpack from the hide and used the sinew for a better bowstring. He dried the meat and carried it in the pack. The deer's stomach was saved for a water bag in case he decided to leave the river. Now that he was better equipped, he felt better.

9.
DESERT

It was another week before he saw signs of humanity. An Indian boy was trying his luck at spear fishing when Yaweta saw him. He waited until the boy had enough fish and headed home. Yaweta followed. He studied the tribe and village from a distance. When it was dark he entered the village, noting the absence of any guards.

The tribe resembled the Cliff Dwellers in that they had huts built of mud and grass. A garden grew close to the river and there were few signs of a warring disposition. He located the chief's dwelling by the markings on the sides and the location in the center of the settlement. Tribes that were prone to war were more mobile than these were so he felt they were probably peaceful. He left the village and went up the river to a place where he had seen a number of deer tracks. In the early morning hours the deer came to drink. Yaweta took two. An hour later he walked into the village with a deer on each shoulder and dropped them in front of the chief's door.

The tribe didn't know what to make of the strange looking man. Some were openly curious while others hid. When the chief appeared Yaweta gave the peace sign and offered the meat as a gift of good will. The chief returned the greeting with a relieved attitude. Although his face did not change expression his body relaxed a little so Yaweta felt he had been tentatively accepted. Yaweta spoke in sign language with the chief and several braves until the evening meal. He learned about the tribe and told the chief about himself.

During the conversation one brave seemed very interested in the medallion around Yaweta's neck. After a few minutes he spoke quietly to the chief and left the circle. In a minute or two he returned with a squaw and the pack Yaweta had when the canoe was capsized. The squaw was wearing one of the medallions. The brave handed the pack to Yaweta and told the woman to give her medallion back. Yaweta stopped her with a gesture. He made a gift of the medallion for the return of his pack. From the pack he presented a silver ring to the brave and one with a turquoise setting to the chief.

The brave had journeyed up the river just to the edge of the canyon tribe's territory. He spotted two men diving into the deep pool at the foot of the rapids near the mouth of the canyon. He came close enough to hear without being seen. They were talking about the power they would have when they found a strange looking big knife. He understood their tongue but had no idea what they were talking about until he had seen Yaweta's sword. The only item they had brought up from the bottom was Yaweta's pack. When the two canyon braves dove into the pool again he took the bag and left. The brave laughed when he told the story and said they were probably still trying to figure out what happened to their loot.

Yaweta's original pack was better than the one he had made out of deer hide so he gave the deer hide one to the brave and put his things in the old one. The turquoise beads, rocks, and most of the jewelry were still in the bag.

He felt right at home with the people so decided to stay a few days. The natives were amazed at the longbow he had made. When he demonstrated it they were impressed at its range. He supplied the tribe with a number of deer and a bear while getting used to his new bow.

In his conversations he learned of a desert to the west and, beyond that, the, "Big Waters That Smell". It had to be the west coast he was seeking. The desert would present a challenge. No one seemed to know just how big it was, since none of them had ever crossed it. They had spent some time out there, and knew the ways of survival. Yaweta was determined to go directly across and find the coast, but not without some preparation.

The natives taught Yaweta how to travel in the desert and how to survive with little food or water. They told him about the water holes they had used and where they were located. He trained by going out into the desert with no food or water a full day and a half and returning. Two braves went with him. He learned to carry a pebble in his mouth to endure thirst, and how to get moisture from a barrel cactus. He learned what to eat and what to avoid. When he was through he felt he could travel the desert with nothing more than a knife.

If he was going to cross the treacherous expanse, even well equipped, he learned to do it at night when it was cool. He moved along at an easy, mile-eating trot, carrying a good supply of food and two water bags. By the time the sun was down and the sky dark, he was well into the desert. He rested until the full moon lighted his way, and then continued through the night. When the sun started heating the desert he found a hole under a sandstone shelf. It was hot, but a lot more comfortable than running in the direct heat. He roused himself out just before sunset, drank some water, and ate his meal. When it started to cool off he trotted away.

As in the previous night he ran at a leisurely pace, stopping occasionally for a sip of water and once for a bite of food. The sky was turning pink with the first signs of morning when a cool breeze began to blow. Half an hour later, sand was blowing in Yaweta's face. To his right was a low sandstone ledge so he turned toward it. He found a wind eroded hollow under the ledge just big enough for him to lie down out of the wind. He lay down and waited for the wind to stop.

The wind picked up. Sand blew over the edge of the ledge, filling the air. Yaweta removed his shirt, wet it, and put in over his face so he would be able to breathe without choking. Breathing was still difficult but sand was not stinging his face and he did not have to fight the wind. Tired from his travels and fairly comfortable, Yaweta slept.

As he slept, he dreamed he was on the ship, but the ship was sinking. Great waves crashed over the small vessel and it slowly sank. As he sank into the water, drowning, he woke up. As the sand blew across the ledge it piled up behind it. The sand piled higher and higher until it started filling the hollow, covering Yaweta. His shirt protected his face but the sand covered him completely and pressed the leather against his nose and mouth. He began to struggle out of the hollow, but when he moved, the sand filled in around him more tightly.

With the last of his strength he got his feet against the sandstone and shoved with all his might. His legs and head were still covered with sand but he felt fresh air across his back. Farther struggling brought his head free. The shirt was lost in the struggle and sand was in his nose so he gasped a large lung-filling volume of air through his mouth and blew it out his nose. This cleared his nose a little. He wiped his eyes as best as he could to get the sand away. Sand got into his eyes anyway.

With tears trying to wash away the foreign substance he could barely see as he dug into the sand pile to recover one of the water bags. This done he rinsed his mouth clear of sand, drank a little, and flushed out his eyes, emptying the bag. With his vision now fully restored he cleared away the sand and recovered his possessions. The second water bag had burst, either from the pressure of the sand or his struggles to get free. He was without water.

His lack of water was of no immediate concern since he had just drank, but would cause a problem later if none was found. He ate some sandy dried meat, adjusted his gear, and moved on. The wind had died down a lot but still stung his face. He used the broken water bag over his head as a mask against the blowing sand. Two very small holes gave him a very narrow but adequate field of vision. The wind had been coming from the west, if it had not shifted while he was sleeping; the right direction would be into the wind, so he started in that direction. Running was out of the question but he moved as rapidly as he could under the circumstances.

Toward sunset the wind ceased. An eerie silence fell over the land. Upon removing his dust mask he saw a range of barren mountains ahead of him. He had been told of a water hole in a cavern at the foot of a tall mountain. Distances in the desert are farther than they appear. Yaweta became grateful for the training he had received. Several times during the night he stopped to cut a plug out of the cactus that gave moisture and wet his lips. When the sun hit him the next day he holed up and waited. Several of the life-saving cactus plants were where he stopped and he partook of them freely. He followed the shade of a particularly large cactus throughout the day. When it began to cool he was off again.

It was almost morning before Yaweta saw the landmark he wanted. The sun had been shining quite a while and his thirst for fresh water was acute when he finally neared the cavern. The water from the cactus was not tasty but it was moisture.

A thin wisp of smoke signaled the presence of someone at the water hole. He knew they probably had already seen him so he didn't try to hide his presence. He was surprised when no one greeted him as he approached.

The water hole was surrounded by willow trees and grass. To one side a garden grew. The water from a pool ran out into the desert and disappeared in the sand after a little distance. The pool was in a large cavern and a permanent camp was set up beside it. As Yaweta came through the willows he saw a girl of about four playing in the stream with a boy of about six. A young brave was sitting by the fire watching as his children played and his squaw prepared a meal. When Yaweta appeared the children ran, screaming in fright, to hide behind their mother. The young brave reached to grab his weapons.

In the dialect of the natives he had left a few days earlier, Yaweta greeted them and raised his arm in the sign of peace. Guardedly they invited him to the fire. After some conversation in sign language, and some words, he saw them relax a little. He passed out pieces of the dried meat as a peace offering.

Kids seem to be able to know when someone likes them. It was not long before the two children were crawling all over Yaweta. They pulled his beard and ran their hands over his chest and arms, laughing and asking why he had hair all over his body. Yaweta laughed with them and explained that all warriors of his tribe were that way. He said he was from a tribe living in the far north and needed hair to keep warm.

The young brave was especially interested in the sword and insisted on trying it out. He could lift it with two hands but could not control its swing. Yaweta showed him how to use the strange weapon by cutting some wood for the fire. The two men talked about the land ahead and where other water holes were located. Yaweta learned there was a lake of salt water to the west, but a stream nearby had fresh water. In hopes that it was the ocean, he asked how big the lake was. The young man said he could walk around it in a day.

The young brave and his family had decided to live away from others of their tribe because there was a difference in philosophy. It was a tribe of vicious people who killed for pleasure. Their raids on other tribes had no purpose, such as gaining territory or food. This young man was not violent, but peace loving and an artist. He displayed his artistic efforts on the walls of the cavern. They were not altogether outcasts from the tribe, but had become guardians of the water hole. From time to time members of the tribe would pass this way.

The mountains were not all sandstone. A short distance up a valley Yaweta found some stones of agate. He took some and proceeded to make an arrowhead. It turned out to be of good quality so he promised to teach the art to the young man. Six months later the young man had the skill mastered. He would be honored by his tribe and the area around his home would be a safe zone for all natives. When Yaweta went on his way he would leave a happy family behind. Twice during the six months members of the tribe came to the camp. Yaweta, as a favor to the young couple, hid himself but he listened to the conversation. He understood enough to know the low esteem the braves had of the young man.

The next time his tribe came by they were surprised when they were shown the arrowheads. When asked how he had learned to make them he had a strange story to tell. A giant white warrior with hair all over his body had shown him the art. He described the strange weapons and the strange metal. He had painted a picture of Yaweta on the cavern wall and made a mud cast of Yaweta's footprint to prove his story. Some of the visiting warriors had heard of Yaweta and his exploits against the fierce Apache. It became well known throughout the area that a great god/warrior had been the teacher.

10.
VISION

Yaweta found the salty lake and the fresh-water stream. As he made his way around the south end of the lake he crossed another stream before turning northwest along the western shore. He had a feeling another stream would enter the lake from this side. He was not disappointed. The water flowed from another barren range of mountains. Several times he saw hunting parties but they avoided any contact with him. Three days after leaving the lake he saw hills with trees on them in the distance. He was so thrilled to see the familiar vegetation he became careless.

As he ran along his foot came down on the back of a rattlesnake. The snake turned and bit him on the ankle. He tied a leather strap around his leg and cut the bite to let the poison drain. He attempted to suck the poison out of his ankle but the bite was at a place he could not reach with his mouth. He was starting to feel weak when he found an overhang beside the stream and made camp. He made himself as comfortable as he could and waited for the poison to take over his body. Before removing the tourniquet he applied a poultice made from leaves and mud to draw out the poison as it dried. Then he relaxed. He ate a big meal of the dried meat he carried, and drank his fill of water. He lay for three days, too weak to move. He passed out and had terrible dreams of burning in fire and freezing in ice.

At first he dreamed he was in a forest. The forest was on fire and he was running as fast as he could toward a lake of water. Then the dream changed and he was walking along a mountain trail. An avalanche came down the mountainside and he was covered by snow, freezing, and clawing his way toward a light. Later the dreams changed.

He dreamed he was in the mountains. Trees were around him and there was a lake of crystal clear water. The place was a valley with big mountains all around the perimeter. Countless deer bear, and other animals were there for his use. He saw small streams with a great many fish, and a large meadow with the deer grazing. The peacefulness of the valley and lack of danger made him feel completely at ease. He walked across the valley and into a tunnel. The tunnel had a bright light at the end. He walked toward the light with a feeling of anticipation and wonder.

He saw himself living in a cave that had a fire coming out of the floor to warm it. The cave was alive with light reflecting from countless jewels, and a pond of warm sparkling water soothed his body. He saw a maiden ministering to his needs. When his dream had him in this setting he was happy.

Sometimes the dreams were not so pleasant. At other times he was in a battle with hostile tribes. Just when he dreamed he was overcome by his foes he would see himself escaping and running. A fierce tribe, of many braves, chased him through the forest. He ran until he felt his lungs would burst and he had trouble getting his breath. He no longer had his sword and his only weapon was a knife. Managing to outdistance his pursuers he ran into a lake during a hard rain. He ran through the water and sought shelter behind some big boulders on the other side. It was then everything became dark and cold. Then he found himself in his valley.

Three days later he became aware of his immediate surroundings. Weakly he got into his pack and pulled out some food to eat. After a while his strength began to return and he was able to drag himself to the stream to drink. He knew he had beaten the poison and would be able to continue his journey after a rest. When he was sure he would be able to travel, he limped away, toward the green hills.

He found the woods and the north end of a small lake with an outlet on the northeast corner. It was an ideal spot to camp for an extended period but the people who were already there had some objections. Yaweta carried a deer into the camp and thought he had done all the appropriate things but he was met by a large group of hostile braves.

The first arrow hit the deer Yaweta had over his shoulder. He knocked another arrow out of the air with his sword and ducked another. The savage natives were too close for comfort when Yaweta gave a loud battle cry and charged, brandishing his sword. The yell had worked before and it worked now. They scattered in all directions. The big man stopped short of killing anyone and retreated to a hilltop nearby. He watched in plain view as the tribe broke camp and left the area, heading south.

Yaweta camped across and down the stream from the old camp. He felt eyes on him less than an hour after his camp was established. Before long he had the two lookouts spotted. In the dark of the moon he circled around and surprised one of them. Both of the watchers had seen Yaweta leave his campfire but lost him in the blackness of the woods. Now he was standing right behind one of them. He laid the blade of his sword on the brave's shoulder. The startled brave turned around quickly and the blade was at his chest. Yaweta motioned him to move down to the fire.

When they arrived at the camp Yaweta invited the brave to sit down. With the sword he cut a large piece of roast venison, stuck it on the point of the blade, and offered it to the brave. Yaweta sat and spoke to him in sign language as though he were an invited guest. After a while the man relaxed and began to communicate. About ten minutes passed before the brave stood and called out. His fellow sentinel came to the fire.

After explaining his strange look and weapons, Yaweta convinced them he was friendly and meant no harm to the tribe. Yaweta learned he had been met with such violence because the camp had been attacked just hours before by another tribe. They had lost some braves and were expecting another attack. There was no way of knowing the raiders had left. Yaweta just happened to walk in at the wrong time. One of the braves acted as a runner to report to his tribe. The next day the village was reestablished on the original site. Yaweta met with the chief and promised his assistance. A few days later it was needed.

A brave was seen spying on the village. That night Yaweta slipped out of camp with the two braves he had befriended. When the morning sun lightened the sky the attack came. Yaweta and his party closed in behind them. His two companions had the job of protecting Yaweta's back. He instructed them to give him plenty of room when he charged. Yaweta's sword cut a wide arc as slashed into the ranks of the attackers. The raiders were caught in a trap and were quickly defeated. The few who escaped had a strange story to tell. There would be no raids on other tribes for a while.

When Yaweta left, his two friends went along as guides. They passed over mountains and through valleys. After having been so long in the desert Yaweta thoroughly enjoyed the journey. It took several days of leisurely travel before they finally came to a beach of sand that stretched for miles along the coast of what the natives had variously called the, "Stinking Waters," or the, "Big Waters That Smell". After more than a dozen years Yaweta had reached the west coast.

11.
EARTHQUAKE

The ocean, that was not yet named Pacific, was peaceful and calm. Waves lapped lazily from the blue water to the smooth sandy beach. The odor of the salt water was offensive to his companions, but brought memories to Yaweta. They set up camp at the mouth of the stream they had been following. Yaweta went down to the beach and dug clams for dinner. It was the first time the Indians had eaten the fruit of the sea and they enjoyed the meal. After a couple days his friends bade farewell and returned to their village.

Yaweta went north along the beach. One week later he was still walking the beach. He couldn't help but wonder what land was on the other side of the ocean. There was no need to hunt or even work very hard he dined on seafood every day. He could see how he could get lazy and fat living on the coast. When he had an urge for red meat there was a variety of animals in the nearby forest. The good weather could not last forever. Rain and wind drove Yaweta into the forest. He built a shelter and waited out the storm.

As he entered the forest he saw signs of a native population. Curious about the people who lived along the coast, he began watching for more signs of habitation. The next day he came across a well-worn path coming out of the forest and leading onto the beach. He found the huts of a village at the end of the path. It was vacant, but Yaweta knew the residents were close. He pretended to leave, but circled around and watched. Eventually the tribe began returning to their homes. They were short, fat, and not at all like the tall, good-looking natives of the plains. He knew they were deathly afraid of him. He was much bigger than they were, his face and body was covered with hair, and he certainly did not speak their language. Everything about him was different from anything they had ever seen.

In the vision of the natives, Yaweta was not human. They saw him as a strange animal. The story of his presence traveled up the coast ahead of him from one tribe to another. The native description was somewhat different from the truth. He was described as an animal that walked upright, and bigger than any bear. His tracks were compared to the small prints and stride left by the tribesmen so they drew their conclusions as to size accordingly. He had to be twice the size of any of them.

Yaweta lost track of time as he wandered north. Not being bothered by Indians except for the occasional one spying on him he relaxed and enjoyed himself. This gave him plenty of time to think. He had long ago given up the idea of reporting back to Captain Mac. The captain and most of the crew had probably died by now. Yaweta felt a stirring within him to find a place he could call home. He had not had one since he was a young lad. However the urge to continue was strong. He knew that one day he would have to settle down but in the mean time he intended to explore this wondrous land as much as he could. He would know when the end of the trail came.

The beach changed to cliffs forcing him inland. The coastline curved round, forming bays and peninsulas. There were rocky beaches and sand beaches. He enjoyed a leisurely trip up the coast. Finally he climbed a high hill. Below him he could see a large inland bay, like a big lake connected to the ocean by a narrow channel. A village was situated just below his vantage point on the shores of the bay. The bay was large enough that He wanted to cross over to the other side of the channel without going around so he decided to see about trading for a canoe.

When Yaweta entered the village the people ran in fright, abandoning everything including a little girl sleeping near one of their dwellings. He sat by their fire for two hours hoping they would come out of the woods where they watched. The little girl finally woke up. She was frightened at first but Yaweta's gentile voice soon calmed her. They began to play. The little girl laughed as she pulled at Yaweta's beard and he ruffled her hair. One of the braves and a squaw cautiously came toward him from the other side of the clearing. The little girl ran to them, chattering away. They grabbed the child and ran.

Yaweta left the two deer he had killed as a peace offering and took one of the canoes that were pulled up on the beach. He paddled away, wishing he had been able to meet the people. He went around and tried to cross the channel that connected the bay to the ocean. The current of the incoming tide caught him and he wound up landing on a rock island in the bay. He paddled around the island and let the current take the canoe into the bay until he could control it better. He was almost to the middle before he could continue. After four hours he completed the trip to the other side of the channel. It was late so he camped for the night.

It may have been the exertion of crossing the channel or because the brave was very good at stealth. Something woke Yaweta in the very early hours of the morning. A brave was pushing the canoe away from shore into the water. Yaweta watched quietly as he climbed in and quietly paddled away. He knew it was the boat's owner, or a member of the tribe. The meat he had left was hanging from the limb of a tree close to where the canoe had been. He cut off a piece and cooked it for

85

breakfast. Two men watched from the shelter of the forest.

If the two spying on him didn't want to be seen or heard, Yaweta felt they probably should not have been wearing seashells. After finishing his meal he broke camp, leaving the rest of the meat. He made a show of leaving and stomped into the woods making noise, breaking limbs, and dragging his feet. After a few yards he circled around and watched as the two men took the food and went back to the trees. He followed them to their canoes and watched as they started away. When they were off shore he stepped out onto the beach, made sure they saw him, and waved. He had never seen two men paddle so fast and look so surprised. The look on their faces made Yaweta laugh.

He took to the ocean shore and continued north. At the end of the day he found a campsite beside a stream. It was a good camp with plenty of game, close to the beach and fresh, clean, water. He stayed a few days before moving on. He wandered inland, still heading north. Eventually he came to a large field. A herd of deer grazed as they migrated to higher ground. Yaweta sat and watched. They reminded him of the herds of another animal he had hunted with the tribe that gave him his name.

After watching awhile he saw the deer suddenly lift their heads as though they had heard something or some smell had come to them. They began milling about in confusion and soon were running in all directions. They were completely panicked. Birds left the trees and took to the air. The forest had a deathly stillness about it. There were no birds singing, and not even insects buzzed or chirped. The air itself felt strange as though something disastrous was about to happen. Yaweta started to stand drawing his sword, to be ready for anything.

As he started to stand he was knocked off his feet. The tree beside where he had been sitting tumbled to the ground, barely missing him. The ground shook as though it were made of jelly. It was impossible to regain his feet as he saw a crack form in the earth and come straight toward him. Not being able to control the situation, his foot went into the crack. The earthquake stopped as quickly as it began. The crack in the earth closed around Yaweta's foot. He dug himself out as he looked around. A number of trees had fallen and on a hillside a dirt slide still tumbled to the bottom of the hill. Yaweta got to his feet, standing on the badly bruised foot.

Walking on the injured limb was painful so he cut himself a walking stick from the branches of the tree and moved into the field. Aftershocks would come and he didn't want to be where trees could fall on him. In a few minutes the ground shook again but not nearly as hard as before. The earth below was getting itself stabilized. He slowly made his way to the banks of a stream and soaked his foot in the cool water. By nightfall the quakes had stopped and he set up his camp on the edge of the forest beside the stream. It was several days before he could walk without pain.

Yaweta became used to using the walking stick. He remembered the staves some people used when he was young, so decided it might be something he could use. A straight willow, just a little longer than Yaweta was tall, became his new tool. When he returned to the ocean beach a few days later he found a large agate and took the time to make a spearhead. The walking stick became a large spear. By now a month had passed and he decided to move on.

When the Dame Mary landed on this land they were impressed by the size of the trees. Two trees would become a load for the ship and be worth a great deal.

Yaweta began to see trees that made them look like twigs in comparison. He was sure just one of these trees would have enough lumber in it to build an entire town. They were so tall they seemed to be holding up the clouds. The bark was a reddish brown color, unlike any tree the explorer had ever seen. He wandered through the woods in total amazement. He had found the giant Sequoia, or Redwood.

Yaweta had been on lakes so big they had tides and surf. He had seen a prairie so large one could travel a week and not reach the other side. There were thousands of acres of grass waving in the wind like ocean waves. He had seen the same prairie covered by strange animals the natives called food of life. He had traveled a river that went on endlessly and was so wide in places he could barely make out the other shore. He had seen lizards bigger than a man and mammoth snakes in a swamp through which it took many days to travel. He had been in an area where it could rain buckets of water one minute and ten minutes later blow dust in your face.

He had been in a canyon so deep it felt as though he were in the heart of the earth. There had been a petrified forest and a desert painted in shades of red, yellow, and brown. He had seen marvels of nature no one in his native land would ever accept as truth. If he told of these things he would be considered insane. Now he was in a forest even he could not believe and he was right there looking at it. He wondered, "Is there any end to the marvels of this land?"

He wandered in the woods, steadily heading north between a range of mountains and the shoreline. The forest of giant trees seemed to go on endlessly. As time passed he was closer to the mountains than the shoreline. The weather began to get colder in the evenings. Yaweta knew it was late in the fall. All the trees that were not evergreens had long since lost their leaves. As the day drew to a close he sought shelter. One of the huge trees had a tepee-shaped hole at the base. He entered and found more than enough room to set up camp inside. The area was larger than any tepee he had ever seen.

In the morning there was a light dusting of snow on the ground. It had been so long since Yaweta had spent a winter in snow country he was caught completely unprepared. The snow caught his attention. The tree was about the best place he would be able to find for shelter. It might need a hide for a door but would be easy to heat. Food and hides would be his first priority. With a forest full of animals it was not difficult to lay in a good supply of both. He began tanning hides to make winter clothing. Along the nearby creek he found a dam made by an animal he had seen before but never knew what it was called. It was almost like a rat with buckteeth and a flat tail. He killed several and made his clothing from their fur. When he wore his new cap, jacket, pants, and boots, he could concede his resemblance to an animal. He was completely covered by the dark brown fur, except his hands and face.

From time to time Yaweta saw Indians scouting his camp. It became almost a daily game spotting the scout. He knew they were learning his routine. When the watchers disappeared for a couple days he changed the routine. Normally he left his shelter in the early morning just after sunup, return about noon for an hour or two, and then leave again until a little before sundown. He decided to exit before full light and scout around. The ploy paid off.

A party of eight braves headed toward his tree. It was not a war party. They had no paint on their faces and were not armed as for war. It was a hunting party. They were out to kill the strange animal roaming in their woods. The animal's den had been sufficiently scouted to learn its habits and the time had come to kill before it harmed any of the tribe. Yaweta watched from the forest as they carefully approached his campsite and entered the tree shelter with weapons ready.

Once they were inside the tree they were surprised to see evidence that the animal had some very human ways. They were talking about it when Yaweta flipped the hide door aside and stood in the entrance. Eight startled braves stared at him. The light of the fire allowed them to see plainly as Yaweta raised his sword and indicated they should sit. Fear, luck, and surprise combined to make the braves comply. Yaweta removed his hat and jacket, keeping a close eye on his guests. Since he had expected company, a large roast was on the fire. Generous portions of the meat were cut each brave was offered a portion at he end of the sword point. With sign language he welcomed them to his home.

In way of introduction he pointed to himself and said, "Yaweta", then pointed to each brave in turn. He learned their names and the meaning of each. They had never heard a word similar to his name so had no thought of its meaning. All native names meant something and had some significance to the individual's life. He told them Yaweta meant Friend of Man, or Protector of the People. The name helped. The braves began asking questions, so Yaweta answered each. He asked his own questions and received answers. No one brought up the subject of the hunting expedition or the mission to kill an animal. They spent the day conversing back and forth. On their invitation Yaweta accompanied the hunting party to their village. If he had not, the braves probably would have been disgraced, or exiled, for lying.

Yaweta had learned that not everything is as it seems long ago. He carried his sword in one hand and the

90

big spear in the other just as a matter of precaution. He was alert to all his surroundings and on guard. As they approached the village they created quite a sensation. Everyone came to meet the hunting party, even before they got to the village. At first they were cheered for capturing the animal. It was cold so Yaweta was wearing all his winter clothes. Fear set in as the "animal" let the braves go forward and lagged behind. He let the braves do all the explaining. Several times natives tried to go around to his back. A look and a rising of the sword put a stop to that. As his new friends talked he heard his name mentioned several times.

He was taken to a long log house to meet with the tribe's leaders. He spoke at length, answering many questions. Eventually the elders seemed convinced he was human. When asked about his origin, he explained, but knew the natives did not have any idea of what he was telling them. With Yaweta's size and obvious existence, they were ready to believe anything he wanted to tell them. He sensed a great fear among the natives. The fear turned into awe.

They offered to make him chief of the tribe. He refused, saying the chief they had was a great and powerful man. He was here to help them if they needed it and only for a visit. They gave him the best place in the long house to sleep and treated him as they would visiting royalty. In the morning gifts were piled on him. He refused all gifts, saying he needed nothing and wanted nothing from them except their friendship.

He returned to his tree with an escort of braves. The winter passed quickly with constant visitors from the village. Every day there would be a number of braves wanting to accompany him on hunting expeditions. With his long-range bow the tribe never lacked for food. He

91

was leading one of the hunting expeditions, in the early spring, when he became immortal.

The grizzly bear may not be the largest bear in the woods, but it is more vicious and plenty big enough. When they first come out of hibernation in the spring they tend to be a little cranky. Yaweta and his party came to a cave along the foot of a cliff. As they approached the cave two grizzly bears attacked the party. Yaweta, being a little ahead of the others, was first to be attacked. The first bear charged on all four feet until just before reaching his foe. Yaweta dropped the point of his big spear to meet the charging bear. It was an automatic action and certainly not planned. The bear's momentum carried it forward. The point entered the bear's chest and the other end of the spear dug into the ground. When the bear stopped the spearhead was showing out his back. Yaweta had no time to see the results.

The second bear was almost on him. He dropped his bow and drew his sword. Just as the bear rose up Yaweta swung and sidestepped, cutting off one of the bear's front feet. Wounded, the bear charged again in rage. Yaweta's sword was better aimed. The bear's skull was split open by the heavy weapon.

He recovered his spear, pulling it on through the carcass, picked up his bow, and left. The rest of the hunters didn't even see him leave. They were busy with the two dead bears and their excitement. When Yaweta found a stream he washed his weapons and decided it was time to move on. He gathered his pack and other belongings from the tree house and left. The braves claimed he had disappeared after disposing of the two bears. It was then they made him one of their gods. He became the god of the hunt and was given a name. The name was best interpreted, Man-Beast God.

Yaweta headed down the stream close to his camp. It led him back to the ocean shore. He headed north along the shoreline. Many days later he was out of the forest of big trees. The mountain range met the coast, forming a barrier of sorts. He walked the shoreline, sometimes waiting for low tide rather than taking the more difficult inland route. In was then he discovered some wreckage. He had seen pieces of board and even a hatch cover, but nothing to indicate what kind of ship.

Now the ocean had delivered a rowboat, with a hole in the side. The boat had been left in the rocks during a storm. Writing on the side was familiar to Yaweta. When he was a young boy he had seen the same hieroglyphics on boxes of raw jade his father had imported from China. It made him wonder if China happened to be on the other side of the ocean. He hauled the craft to a place safe from high tide and made repairs by using bark and pitch. He built oars similar to the paddle he had made long ago from branches and leather.

With oarlocks made from forked branches and the new oars, he traveled the ocean rather than the land. As long as he stayed out far enough to get away from the surf he could move along quite well. At night he would go up a stream or inlet to camp away from the constant wind along the ocean beach.

Every now and again Yaweta had seen totem poles in villages and in other places. He came across one with a different figure. There were the usual depictions of man, beast, and bird, but this one had a fish as the primary figure. As the days passed he saw others, usually in groups of three, with the fish. He came to a village and entered. The natives had heard of him from the tribe he had visited so were not afraid, only cautious. They wondered why a god was visiting them. They even showed him his totem and asked his approval of the carving. He agreed it was a sufficient likeness.

Sometimes one learns by keeping his mouth closed. Yaweta didn't ask questions about the fish on his totem or the other totem poles. When mealtime came he was served a very large portion of fish. From the size of the piece of meat he couldn't wait to see a whole one. He got his wish the next morning. He accompanied the men to the nearby river to fish. They were spearing fish as fast as they could. The water was filled with the largest fish Yaweta had ever seen. In this land, where everything seemed big, it didn't surprise him to find the fish were also big. To get an idea of the size he took one and held it out at arm's length. It was so heavy he could barely keep it up long enough to find it was longer than his legs. There were others even longer.

The fishermen saw him getting the heft and length and thought he was approving of their occupation. Not one of them could hold a fish out at arms length and look at it so easily. Like most natives he had found on the coast, these were also short and fat. At first Yaweta thought they were quite lazy, in comparison to the other tribes he had visited. They didn't even use points on their spears. All they had to do was to sharpen the end to a point. There was no need for hard work and exercise because everything they needed was provided by the sea. He learned how lazy they were when he went fishing with some of the tribesmen. Sometimes it took two men to pull one fish out of the water. Yaweta tried it himself. It was hard work.

One evening, when he stopped for the night, he entered a long inlet. He set up a camp there to use as a base. He had seen gigantic dunes of almost pure white sand and wanted to look them over. The dunes seemed to go on endlessly and stretched inland as high, white hills.

There were ponds formed by the dunes and Yaweta began to wonder how they had been filled with water. He found out.

12.
TIDAL WAVE

He learned about storms along the coast of this ocean the hard way. He had camped, he thought, a sufficient distance up the inlet from the salt water. After a meal of the big fish he settled in for the night with a bearskin wrapped around him. During the night he was awaken by a strange feeling of danger. He got his things together and was just beginning to move inland when the tidal wave hit. He had thought about the storm on the southern coast and figured he was in for another one because the air felt the same. The wind was blowing off the water and picking up speed.

A wall of water, nearly as high as the trees around him, came crashing over the beach. Yaweta barely had time to get behind a big tree and hang on with all his strength. The wave covered him and continued until it broke against a hillside. He was under water and thought he was going to drown so he started climbing the tree, more swimming than climbing. The water receded almost as fast as it had come ashore. The man was left clinging to a limb high up in the tree. He saw trees fall into the water and float back toward the ocean.

The tree to which he clung went over. Yaweta rode it down and was still riding it when it was dragged back toward the sea. As the water dropped some of the branches hung up on the rocks along the shoreline, snapping the tree in two. A second wave, smaller than the first, caught the pieces and threw them back toward the shore. Stunned, Yaweta clung to a piece of the trunk. The wave lifted him high. The wood was about to crash to the ground when he desperately reached out, grabbing a branch on another tree. This one was still standing.

Looking down he spotted a small patch of sand among the logs and rocks. He dropped down and ran inland. Three more waves followed, each less severe than the previous one. Eventually the sea calmed to a regular summer storm.

Yaweta surveyed the damages. He found his spear under a large boulder. The point was good but the rock had broken the lance. If the rock had not held it down he would have lost it all. His pack with all its treasures was on his back but filled with saltwater. The food was ruined. The beads and raw turquoise survived but the silver would have to be washed with clean water right away before the salt water corroded the metal. The same was true of his sword and knife. Naturally the rowboat was gone, probably broken to bits. When daylight found him he was deep in the woods. He would have to replace his bearskin robe and some of his other things. Everything else needed a good washing.

He had camped beside a stream so he followed it away from the ocean. He found a deep pool at the foot of a waterfall. It was a beautiful location so he took the time to set up a camp. The fresh water took care of the salt that would ruin everything and the warm sun dried the leather and furs that remained. He built himself a lean-to and went hunting. He was tired of fish.

He found the meat he needed in the woods. He went back to his new camp and built a fire to cook his meal. The smell of the food attracted visitors. A boy and a girl of about ten summers wandered into camp. They were obviously afraid of him but they were more concerned about something else. The boy took him by the hand and pulled, trying to get him to follow. Neither child spoke and Yaweta sensed it was because of shock. Something was very wrong so Yaweta went along.

As they traveled he looked the children over. They had obviously been caught in the tidal wave. They were badly bruised and had abrasions on their arms and legs. Both seemed to be able to walk and used their arms well, so he thought they were not the worse for wear. They came to a small clearing along the stream. He could see the devastation caused by the wave reaching this far inland. A camp had been there but there was nothing left worth saving. A man was dead with a branch sticking out of his chest. The woman was in better shape but was being held down by a fallen tree. It took all his strength to lift the trunk away so she could be freed. She had a broken arm, several cuts, and was badly bruised. Yaweta cleaned her cuts and set her broken limb. She screamed with pain as he pulled the arm and gently put the bones back in place. He then made a splint and tied it on with leather. He used sinew to sew some of the worse cuts. She passed out from the pain, but he was able to stop the bleeding so she would not bleed to death. He carried her back to his camp. There he built another, larger lean-to for his guests.

The woman did not know where she was. She had a bad fever and was unconscious, but when he felt for her pulse, she was alive. He bathed her in the clean water to keep the fever down and the wounds clean. When he went hunting he instructed the children how to care for her. He was never gone very long but he provided four bearskins for bedding and several deer hides for clothing. He had very little sleep for several days but the woman finally broke the fever and was awake. When she saw Yaweta she was frightened until the boy and girl talked to her and calmed her down.

Yaweta gave her clothes to wear when he felt she had enough strength to move about the camp. She understood his sign language so they talked. She had family in a village some distance away so Yaweta volunteered to take them there when she was well enough to travel. A month later she had healed. There were some bad scars, but her arm seemed to have healed properly. She was different from the normal Indian he had seen along the coast. She was taller, quite slim, and had an abundance of energy. The family had been from a tribe living inland and had only come to the ocean for the seashells. They had value in trading with other inland tribes.

When they finally left he had replaced everything he lost to the wave except the boat. They headed north by northeast for several days. Yaweta noticed mountain ranges both to the east and to west. Since he had reached the west coast he noticed the mountains becoming more and more rugged. It was natural to wonder how big the range was. Many times in the past dozen or so years he thought he would give anything for a horse. Now he wished even more for such an animal. In all his travels he had never seen one. He assumed they were not native to this land or he would have seen one by now.

It took over a week of leisurely travel through tree-covered hills and valleys that always had a stream. The two kids were a total joy to the big man and their mother, though weak, was a good traveler. Yaweta had not enjoyed himself so much in years. It created a feeling in him he did not recognize. It was a vague longing for something more than exploration and wandering.

They broke out of the woods along the banks of a crystal-clear lake. A wide trail led to the village of her people. The village, and the setting, reminded him of another one, long ago, where he had adopted a son. The woman was the daughter of the chief. They were welcomed with great joy and celebration.

For a change, the tribe accepted him as a man and didn't ask all the tedious questions. He gained somewhat of a reputation as a medicine man because of his treatment of the woman. Fortunately they never brought him any patients. He thoroughly enjoyed the companionship, acceptance, and the freedom. He made friends rapidly and accompanied them on many hunting trips. His longbow contributed to their larder frequently so he became well respected. The tribe used arrowheads of flint on their arrows but the points were in short supply.

Without an arrowhead maker in the area they had to travel a great distance to obtain the necessary item. Yaweta searched and found agates. He showed how the stone would make a good point, using his spear point as an example. Being harder than flint, making an agate arrowhead took a lot of time. He decided to seek an easier way.

He moved his residence up a valley to have more privacy and so he wouldn't look so much like a fool when his experiments failed. He tried various ways to cut the stone. He was able to split the agates and break off pieces but to make an acceptable arrowhead; finish work had to be done. He thought about a method used when he was an apprentice. He called it cracking. He sought the hot metal used by his father to accomplish the task.

He needed two things - coal and lead. Coal would make a fire hot enough to melt and heat the lead. The lead would be used to make the finished product. After a month of exploration he found galena. Galena is lead in its natural state. One of the braves showed him an outcropping of coal after he described the substance to him. The people of the tribe did not understand how he could burn rocks to melt other rocks. Once the coal caught fire and the lead started melting he had created quite a marvel among them. He built a fire and piled coal on it. When the coal was burning brightly he piled big chunks of galena on top. The lead melted and formed pools in the hot coals. A long sliver of rock was used to dip in the hot lead and onto the agate. All his training as a jeweler and arrow maker was put to the test. There were many failures but his method was finally sufficiently effective. Summer ended, and winter came twice before Yaweta had produced all the arrowheads and spearheads the tribe would need for years.

It was springtime when he finally decided to leave. He was told the river from the lake went to a larger one, and then to one even bigger. The chief told him about the route and portages he would need to make. They outfitted him with a canoe and two young braves were sent along as helpers until he was at the second river. He bid the tribe a fond farewell, leaving behind good friends. The two young men helped him around waterfalls and rapids as they left the mountains and entered a large valley. The river joined another larger one just as promised. They camped a couple days. Yaweta gave the last of his jewelry to his helpers and sent them home. He still had some stones, beads, and arrowheads of turquoise. Most of his arrows had agate points, as did his new, oversized, spear.

Drifting down the river made a slow journey and gave him plenty of time to enjoy himself and the scenery. Since it was spring the big fish were thick in the water. Their backs were red, with white sections, but it was the same fish as the one the coastal tribes used. The natives had told him all about the spawning cycle and informed him that the fish was not good to eat at this stage. Time slipped away and the man covered a good distance each day even though he had not tried to hurry. It was only a few days before he reached a much larger river. This one flowed from the east toward the westward ocean.

13
EGGS OF THE GODS

It was the largest river he had seen since the big river he and Sojata had traveled to the south years ago. If it was anything like the previous one it had to be a very long river. He wondered how close it would take him to the lake where he had started. It was an interesting idea. If there was a passage to the lake it would be conceivable to establish a link to the ocean. If, in truth, China was on the other side of the western ocean, the result would be a much shorter route to the oriental trade from Erin. Captain Mac would certainly be interested if he was still alive. It occurred to him that if this river did go that far, Captain Mac and the crew might be at the mouth. He decided to look.

Turning his canoe west he traveled to the mouth of the river and explored the area. He saw several villages but no sign of his friends. After a few days he decided they had never gotten this far west. It did not surprise him. One thing Yaweta had learned well: Never be surprised by anything in a land where so many things were bigger than the imagination and the impossible was normal. He turned the canoe east, paddling close to shore to avoid the strong current as he went upriver. He passed the point of his entry into the river and proceeded east.

To the north were two enormous mountains and to the south another. The mountains around them were high and rugged but these three stood way above anything around them. The peak of each was obscured by clouds. Later in the day he could see the snow-covered peaks. One to the north had smoke, or steam, rising from a fissure close to the top. He had used the southern mountain as a guide for a long time and felt some fondness for it.

When he stopped that evening he heard the sound of falling water. He made camp in a grotto at the foot of a tall waterfall. The surroundings were so pleasant he stayed a couple days. He swam in the pond and stood under the falls. For the first time in years he felt like singing. He remembered an old Irish ballad and sang with enthusiasm. Later, when he went hunting for supper, there was not an animal in the woods. He caught some fish out of the stream, for his evening meal.

The hills fell behind him and he found himself at the edge of a great prairie. The banks of the river were high and he could only occasionally see beyond them. He camped on the south bank in a small grove of trees. The next morning he explored. He found he was on the east side of the mountain range. He climbed the foothills. To the east was a vast, barren, prairie with rolling hills as far as he could see. He went a little farther south along the foothills until he climbed a slope that would give him a better view. He was sure this could not be the western edge of the plains he had hunted years ago because in the distant haze he could see another range of mountains. They formed a jagged blue line between the earth and the sky. Even from this great distance they looked large.

While there he found rocks shaped somewhat like eggs. He collected several after finding one that was cracked. When he broke it open he found it was a hollow agate. The inside was lined with crystals. He broke a half dozen of them. All had hollow centers but each was different. The heaver ones had less of a hollow. They were nice, pretty, and interesting, but useless, unless they had plenty of agate. He took some of the heaver ones with him on the assumption they might be solid.

As he approached his campsite, after a two-day absence, he saw three men in his camp. They were loading their canoe and his belongings. He could only assume they thought whoever had camped there would never be back. They were so intent on the loading that Yaweta was standing close by when they saw him. Three startled braves stood there, open-mouthed. Yaweta said nothing, just pointed his spear at the canoes and then moved it to the campsite. They got the idea quickly and moved to put everything back where they had found it. When they were through he pointed his spear from them to their canoe and out into the river. They climbed aboard and paddled away rapidly. He could hear them talking and knew they were discussing him as they moved.

Since the braves had gone upstream he knew that the news of his existence was going ahead of him. This had generally worked to his advantage and he hoped this time would not be an exception. In the next few days he saw people several times, but always on the other side of the river. They waved to him as though they were friends. He saw them often enough to know they were keeping an eye on him.

He came to a place where a smaller river entered. There were woods and a village at the location. He camped near them. The Indians feared him and would not approach the strange man. A line of warriors formed a barrier between him and the village. Yaweta was never one to stay where he was not welcome. He left at the first light of morning. It had looked as though it would rain so he had built a lean-to for shelter. The small trees and limbs he needed were easy to cut with his sword and it didn't occur to him that anything was unusual. He pushed his canoe into the river and looked back as he paddled away. He saw the men inspecting the smooth cuts made by his blade. An hour later he caught sight of a runner on

105

the north shore. He was heading upriver at a fast pace. There was either a welcome or an ambush up ahead.

Gradually the river turned in a great arc toward the north. He came to a place where another small river entered. Again, a tribe was living there. He was welcomed like a long-lost brother. To Yaweta's way of thinking everything was a little too much. They were a little overenthusiastic with the welcome. They threw him a big feast with elaborate welcoming speeches, but they seemed to have no interest in having him speak. The tepee they gave him to use was back in the trees, away from everyone and the beach. He went to bed a little apprehensive. He remembered the overly friendly tribe in the canyon. They had tried to drown him.

Twice his sixth sense caused him to wake suddenly. He could see no reason for the danger signal so he dozed off again. The third time it happened he noticed that his pack was missing. He lay still, fully alert and ready. The tepee was small so his spear poked outside under the edge. His sword was also close to the edge with the blade touching the side. He felt his spear moving slowly out of the tepee. His sword started moving right before his eyes. The blade moved under the tepee and slowly disappeared under the edge. There was no sound or sign of a person but the weapons were still moving.

Yaweta grabbed both weapons. He shoved the spear straight out they yanked it back. He felt the point strike flesh and heard a yelp of pain. At the same time he wrapped his fist around the handle of the sword and twisted it around, shoving at the same time. Another cry of pain proved the tactic effective. With the sword in one hand and dragging the spear, point down, in the other, he leaped out of the entrance flap. As he came out of the tepee two braves rushed him. He shoved the sword and the butt of the spear forward. The sword went into the

106

stomach of one brave and the spear handle broke the windpipe of the other.

By now his war cry ripped through the air. Two more members of the tribe charged him and were quickly sent to their reward. The rest of the tribe ran like the sneak thieves they were. Yaweta recovered his pack and packed his gear in the canoe. He trashed their camp piling everything up including their canoes and set it on fire. He wanted to send a different message ahead - a message that warned, "Don't mess with Yaweta".

He had gone only a little distance when he saw four canoes pulled up on the riverbank. Twelve braves stood watching him from the shore. He could see their war paint by the light of the moon. Yaweta noticed a difference in their dress but just in case they were of the tribe of thieves he went past them without hesitation. The braves got in their canoes and followed. They never tried to catch him, only follow. They were less than a bowshot behind yet never showed a sign of hostility. When evening came they were still there. Yaweta spotted the perfect place to camp. He spotted a cave on the side of a cliff. There was a small level spot in front and a rockslide reaching to the water.

When he docked his canoe he found a trail of loose rocks waiting. To the amazement of his followers he picked up the loaded canoe and carried it up the steep incline. The small rocks slipped and rolled under his feet but he did not stumble. He set the canoe down on the level spot and looked inside the cave. It was not suitable for his bed but would be handy in case of rain. He camped beside the boat. He ate a mixture of dried meat and berries and settled in for the night. His followers went on up the river.

The sun was just appearing over the horizon when he heard footsteps on the loose rocks. Looking down he saw two natives approaching. Their canoe was docked but the other three canoes were standing offshore, loaded with their ten companions. One brave had a rabbit in each hand. The other one carried an armload of wood for a fire. Yaweta signaled to them with a wave of his hand and they came up the incline. One built a fire while the other prepared the rabbits for cooking. While the meal was cooking they introduced themselves. The other braves were not asked to come ashore. There was not enough room for everyone on the level spot and Yaweta was still wary.

They were, as Yaweta suspected, a war party. They had been sent to punish the thieving tribe for an offence against their village. When they arrived they saw the devastation Yaweta was dishing out and decided he had done their job for them. In trying to steal from the big man they had lost everything, including four dead and two wounded. They expressed some surprise at Yaweta's lack of looting the camp before leaving. He explained his thoughts on the subject. If he took their things, would he be any different from the thieves?

After the meal and cleanup they all traveled together. In camp at night they played at showing off their skills. The natives were good when it came to the games but Yaweta still beat them. He thought it was because he was the guest. They threw knives at targets, shot arrows for accuracy and distance, and had a spear-throwing contest. The shorter bows of the natives were no match for the longbow of Yaweta. The spear throw was more competitive. Yaweta's heavy spear went the same distance but no farther than the lighter spears of the natives. When the contests were over Yaweta left his steel knife sticking in the tree as though he had forgotten it was there. Later in the evening one of the braves brought it to him, scolding him good-naturedly for leaving his tools lying around.

The next day the sun was high in the sky when they came to a fork where two rivers came together to form one. The tribal home was at the fork between the two rivers. Since both rivers were about the same size, it was impossible to tell which the main stream was. It was a large village with hundreds of families. Most of their food came from the water but there were a number of hunting expeditions up the rivers, and tributaries, to obtain furs and red meat. Yaweta always went along. They built rafts to float their game back to the settlement. Yaweta learned the area well enough to decide he wanted to take the river leading to the northeast when he left in the spring.

One evening he was cleaning his pack and organizing things. He laid the egg-shaped agates he was carrying to one side. One of the braves saw them and exclaimed about their value. Yaweta was told the tribe held them in great esteem. The tribe considered them eggs of the gods. Yaweta spent his spare time during the winter polishing some of the eggs. Once they were polished he split two of them to expose the inside.

Spring was there before he finished the project and presented the stones to the tribe. He could not have given a better gift. It was the same to them as giving bags of gold to a poor man back in Erin.

He left with a big send-off and a companion who carried a message for another village of the same tribe upriver. The river twisted and turned like a snake, making the journey longer than an overland route would have taken. They turned up another small river and found the village by a high waterfall. Young children were enjoying themselves in the pool at the base of the falls. He found the location to be one of peace and tranquility.

14.
FIRE

He was told of the journey ahead and of a deep canyon where the river could not be traveled. He was told of a trail leading northeast that was traveled by the natives when they went to trade with another tribe that lived by a big lake. Yaweta decided to take the trail. He was given a rundown on the natives he would likely meet on the trail and the ones who lived on the shores of the lake. A few days up the winding river made him glad to leave its rough waters and send his friend back to his own people.

It was not a trail through the prairie or a desert. This trail twisted up, over, around, and between hills and mountains. It was sometimes easy, sometimes rough, but it was always beautiful. He came to valleys with lakes that vaguely reminded him of something but he could not pin it down. It took an uneventful month of leisure travel to reach the big lake.

Yaweta came out of the woods to the shore of the lake. His first thought was about the Indian's idea of big lakes. This one was not even close to big in Yaweta's estimation. The thing that surprised him most was the lack of a village. There had been a rather large settlement at the place where he stood. By the heat of the coals of the fires there had been people in the place not an hour earlier but the whole village had been moved. They must have been in a big hurry. The site had not been cleaned as it normally would have been. This place was a mess. Things that normally would have been taken with them were scattered about. The signs showed that there had been a hasty exit by canoe.

The wind shifted and Yaweta smelled the reason for the hasty exit - smoke. At first he thought it was from the cook fires but it was too strong. Looking up he saw a grey cloud to the north. He had been traveling in deep woods for the past two days and had not reached any high points of view. The smoke told him there was a forest fire. The wind was pushing it straight toward him. He went south along the lake but the fire was catching him. The only escape was in the water but he had no boat.

Using his sword he cut down a tall slim tree, cut two long lengths, and lashed the two logs together. By the time the tree had been cut down he could hear the explosions of trees bursting into flames at the front of the fire. He had just finished lashing the logs together and tying his belongings to them when the fire raced through the tops of the trees over his head. He could see the lower fire when he launched his makeshift boat. The heat and smoke was unbearable. He felt he was burning as he pushed away from shore. With smoke in his eyes he could barely see and his lungs ached for fresh air. He coughed and choked his way free. He bent down and paddled with his hands until he was clear. Once away from the shore the wind took the smoke away and he could breathe again. He sat up and looked back. The place he had been was completely engulfed in flames. He paddled slowly toward the opposite shore.

From the other shore the tribe watched as the fire swept through their home of generations. They would have little trouble establishing a new location on this side of the lake but a sense of loss caused them to be sad. As they watched the fire they witnessed a strange-looking creature straddling two logs exit the fire. From their vantage point it looked as though he came right out of the fire rather than from in front of it. He was heading straight toward the place where they stood. Their attention was taken from the fire and focused on the man.

When Yaweta got close to shore his spear made a good push pole. As he reached the bank the people backed away giving him plenty of room. The water was only knee deep when he dismounted and walked ashore. For the sake of safety he drew his sword casually as though it was a normal thing. When his feet touched dry land he stopped. A sign of friendship broke the ice. He already knew this tribe was not prone to violence. They were traders, used to seeing strange tribes and a variety of people. They had never seen anyone quite like this one. He was not only strange looking; they thought he had come out of the fire without being burned. He told how he escaped the flames several times before he convinced them he was not impervious to fire.

Representatives of several tribes were there. The tribe traded arrowheads and spear points for the other things they needed. Yaweta was able to learn about many other tribes because he stayed in the village until late summer. He listened to tales of the various trails they had taken so he could learn about the area. Another much larger lake lay to the north, and yet another beside the big mountains.

When they talked about the big mountains he knew exactly what they meant. He could see them, still blue in the distant horizon to the east but much closer. They formed a north-to-south barrier across the land. The snow-covered mountain range was a great distance away but even from here he could tell the peeks were higher than anything he had thus far encountered. He remembered the three peeks. This whole range looked as high as those three sentinels. The mountains drew him toward them like a siren of the deep drawing sailors to their doom. He hoped it was not for the same reason.

The leaves on some of the trees were beginning to turn yellow when he decided to leave. The next morning he headed north toward the second lake. A brave from the tribe who lived there accompanied him. They traveled over mountains where they could look down into canyons with silver streams running through them. At times they went through valleys and walked beside a mountain stream or river with mountains on both sides. In a few days they arrived at their destination. While visiting the tribe Yaweta happened to pull two arrowheads out of his pack, one turquoise, and one agate. The chief was quite taken with the unusual points. He offered Yaweta a tame wolf, broken to pack, in trade. By the time the trade was completed the explorer had the wolf, some bear robes, snowshoes, and a tepee. The chief had several of the special arrowheads and had his squaw sew them on his ceremonial shirt as jewelry.

When Yaweta showed an interest in the medicine man's profession the man began to teach him everything he knew about using natural medicines. Yaweta was a good student, eager to learn. Eventually, he was accorded the honor of being the medicine man's assistant and even took care of some patients.

He made friends with the women and learned how to make the winter food used by the tribe. They mixed berries and meat together, pounded the mixture thoroughly, until it was a thick paste, and laid it out on stones to dry. The mixture was quite nourishing. He learned which berries and roots were good to eat and how to prepare them. Between the medicine man and the women he learned much.

After spending so much time with women Yaweta was looked upon as somewhat of a big sissy. Some of the people began to treat him without respect. Many asked why he wanted to be a woman. He tried to explain that he traveled alone and needed to learn all things in order to survive. Instead of understanding, they tried to get him married. Yaweta refused to court any of the daughters.

This hurt his reputation even more. When the time came that he had learned all he wanted to know he decided it was time to redeem himself in the eyes of the braves.

15.
THE RACE

It was nearing time for the tribe's annual games. In the spring of each year the tribe held contests of skill. It served as a tune-up for the braves after a long winter. When he asked to join the contest there were those who laughed. The chief gave permission and the laughter soon turned to amazement and admiration.

The first event was the throwing of knives for accuracy and distance. After much elimination it was between Yaweta and one brave. The winner would be the champion. The brave threw his flint knife to tie Yaweta at twenty strides. Each time they tied the target was moved back another pace. Yaweta had the target moved back another twenty paces and threw. His knife stuck in the center of the target. His competitor's knife fell short of the mark by two paces.

During the bow and arrow competition Yaweta's arrows went farther and straighter than any other did. Even when they tried moving targets he won. When it came to wrestling or tests of strength he had no equal. Yaweta was the ultimate warrior. He won every event with ease, until the last one.

The last event was a cross-country race. The course went up a long valley, along a ridge, and down another valley. It included everything from flat country running to mountain climbing. Forty braves, including Yaweta, started out on the two-day run. The rules were simple - finish the run. Stopping to rest or eat was optional. They traveled light with as few clothes as possible, a knife, and an extra pair of moccasins. Most runners carried a piece or two of the dried food for energy. It would never occur to one of them to cheat in any way.

The race started on a signal from the chief at first light. Some started fast, to gain a big lead, before slowing down for the long run. Others started more slowly to conserve their strength for the end. Yaweta's easy pace carried him ahead of all but a few. He had learned how to pace himself years earlier when he crossed the desert. He covered the flat ground and proceeded up the valley, passing runners as he went.

One young brave stayed ahead of him throughout the day. Yaweta rested when it became dark and started again when the moon lighted the way. The young brave had done likewise. He was still ahead by about the same distance. When morning came they were alone on the trail. Everyone else was far behind. When the moon disappeared Yaweta rested again. He started out once more when he could see where his feet were falling. His competitor had gained a little and was a couple minutes in the lead.

The trail went over rocks, up the side of a mountain, and across streams. Before entering the final valley it crossed a ridge along the edge of a cliff. The trail narrowed. There were big rocks to one side and a shear drop on the other. It was there that the front-runner ran into trouble. As he rounded a turn he ran headlong into a brown bear. A swipe of the bear's paw ripped through the young brave's lower leg and threw him back. He landed in the middle of the trail.

Yaweta saw the young man as he disappeared around the turn ahead and saw him bounce back as though he had ran into a brick wall. The bear was making a second attack when Yaweta arrived. He stood over the young man and watched as the big brown bear rose to his back legs and walked toward him. Yaweta charged. He

116

bent down and threw himself against the animal. The force of his charge knocked the bear over.

Yaweta picked himself up from the trail where he had landed after the impact. The bear rolled as his back hit the ground and recovered more quickly. Yaweta was still in the process of standing when the bear charged again. Instead of continuing to stand Yaweta dropped to his back. As the bear came over him he put his feet on the bear's body and pushed with all his strength. The lifting motion and the momentum of the bear's charge carried him over the man and through the air, riding on the strong legs of the white native. The arc carried the bear over the edge of the cliff.

The young brave's leg was bleeding profusely. The leather string of a medicine bag that was around the man's neck worked as a tourniquet, but without medical aid he would bleed to death. Yaweta knew what to do but did not have the materials to sew and dress the wound. He threw the young brave over his shoulders and took off running at top speed. There was no stopping to rest. Time was of the essence. The urgency of the situation and a burst of adrenalin made Yaweta's feet fly. The two-day run was completed in just over a day and a half. Yaweta carried his burden across the finish line and directly to the medicine man's tepee. He aided the native doctor in sewing and dressing the wound before he collapsed from exhaustion.

Both Yaweta and the young brave were at the finish when the first of the other braves arrived. When all runners were accounted for the ceremony honoring the winner began. The chief was about to announce Yaweta as the one when the white man drew him aside. In the Indian language the winner of the race was the first brave whose feet crossed the line. There was no mention in the rules of how those feet should cross. Yaweta pointed out that when he carried the young man across the line his feet had been sticking forward. The young brave was declared the winner. To Yaweta's way of reasoning he had been ahead when the bear stopped him and probably would have been ahead at the finish line.

While the young runner recovered from his wound Yaweta saw to his needs. As they talked, he told Yaweta about a forest of giant trees. When the young man could travel again they went to look at the forest. It was to stretch out and strengthen the wounded leg. Yaweta's tame wolf was with them. He pulled a travois with extra supplies.

They came to a forest of very large trees Yaweta recognized as cedar. They were very large but not nearly as huge as some of the trees he had seen on the coast. They camped a couple days before separating. Yaweta went to explore in the general direction of the big mountains and the young brave returned to his home.

16.
AVALANCHE

Yaweta followed the mountain game trails through endless evergreen forests. His general direction was toward the big mountains as he went over hills, up streams, and into valleys. Although his ultimate goal was the mountains he was in no hurry. He was enjoying the serenity and scenery of the trail.

One day he found a stream that interested him. Large, brown backed, trout with a red fringe around the gills lay in the pools waiting for food to come their way. He was looking forward to fish for dinner as he followed it upstream. The valley began to narrow and the trail beside the stream went around a big boulder at the side of the hill. It was there Yaweta came face to face with danger in the form of the largest animal in the forest, and certainly the largest animal he had ever seen.

He had thought the shaggy-headed beasts of the plains were big when he helped hunt the great herds. This one was much bigger and had horns that spread out into a massive rack with wicked points. He had seen pictures of this one when he was a boy but did not realize how very large they were. It was called an elk in the books of his childhood (today it is called a moose in America).

During one time of the year, rutting season, the Bull Moose is very dangerous and will attack anything that moves. This happened to be that time of year. The animal snorted and lowered its head to charge. The horns seemed to reach out to gather the giant warrior to his doom. As the moose charged Yaweta dodged to the side and had already started climbing a shale slide that came down beside the big boulder next to the trail when the animal charged again.

That same rock had shielded Yaweta's vision so he had not seen the animal until it was too late. He reached the top of the boulder using his spear to help maintain his footing. The tame wolf was not so fortunate. It was difficult for him to get out of the way because of the travois he was pulling. A spike of one horn entered the animal's rib cage. Both the travois and the wolf were thrown through the air. The animal was dead before it hit the ground on the other side of the stream.

The second charge was stymied by the loose shale but the moose was not going to give up. He charged the boulder. The rock shook under the impact and moved under Yaweta's feet. As the animal backed away and started prancing around, waiting for him to come down, or trying to figure a way to get to him, Yaweta regained his footing and took stock of his situation. The moose raised his head and bellowed. Seeing his chance Yaweta threw his spear as hard as he could.

The spear buried itself deep in the animal's flesh between the neck and the shoulder. The moose was hurt but by no means dead. He seemed to become more violent than before. As he passed the boulder Yaweta jumped onto his back, sword in hand. With both arms, and a mighty swing, the big man struck the moose squarely between the horns, splitting the animal's skull. Yaweta scrambled to get away as the animal dropped like a rock.

With all the fresh meat and the hide to tan Yaweta decided to seek a good campsite. The project would take some time. Just a short walk farther up the stream, he passed through a narrow passage to a beautiful basin.

A small lake was at the head of the stream he had been following. The forest around the lake was alive with animals. Near the outlet of the lake a cave beckoned him to move in. He set up his headquarters, moved his kill

120

into the camp, and built the racks needed to cook, smoke, and dry the meat.

While processing the meat he tanned the moose hide and wolf fur. The moose leather made the best pair of moccasins he had ever owned. He made several pair, including some with rabbit-fur linings for use in the winter. The wolf made a fur coat. He used a large part of the moose leather to construct a reflector to push heat from his campfire into the cave. Snow was on the ground before the meat preparation and tanning was completed. He thought that this would be a good place to spend the winter.

When Yaweta killed the moose he had an audience. Two braves on a hunting expedition were across the stream high up on the hillside. They could not see clearly through the trees and the natural haze created by the stream. They thought they had seen a fight between two animals. They recognized the moose but the other animal was strange to them. With all the hair on its body and its large size, it could not be a brave although it did act like a man. It was not a bear. They would recognize a bear. They concluded that the animal was half-human and half bear, or some new species never seen before and living in the basin. The location of the fight was significant because the basin was considered a mystic place. No native would enter there. Yaweta did not know of the superstition but soon learned the reason. Tales of the man-beast spread throughout the tribes. Once more Yaweta was considered something more than what he was, a man.

The soil at the entrance of the basin was rich in phosphorous. During the night an eerie glow from rotten wood chips and even some of the rocks at the entrance gave the area a frightening luminescence. When Yaweta first saw it he was startled. On investigation he recognized the substance from his youth, so he thought no more about it than the wood and soil that contained it.

For fun, he arranged some of the rotting wood and rocks in a pattern to spell his name at the entrance. The letters were strange indeed to the natives and were interpreted by their medicine men as an omen of evil. They predicted that the beast living there would come out and destroy everyone unless they could kill it first. The medicine men promised that the warrior who found a way to take the beast's life would be very powerful.

Heavy wet snows piled high on the mountains and in the basin. Yaweta put his snowshoes to use many times foraging for fresh meat and wood. If it was not for the prepared meat of the moose he would have gone hungry many times. During one of the few warm spells Yaweta was hunting on the side of one of the mountains surrounding the basin. As he followed a rabbit track he heard a loud rumble above him. His first reaction was to draw his sword. He turned to face whatever had made the noise when the first of the avalanche hit him.

He was knocked from his feet and rolled down the hill along with trees, rocks, and soil. He never lost consciousness but he did lose his sword and spear as well as all sense of direction. The avalanche was over in seconds. Yaweta was battered, bruised, and under a great pile of snow.

As his mind became reorganized he felt the pain of the bruises he had sustained. It was then he realized he was completely disorientated. The snow was packed around him as he struggled to gain room. Before long he had made enough of a hollow to move his arms. He dug in the snow above his head, not knowing which direction he was digging. Like an earthworm he moved slowly through the snow. He found that the snow had trapped enough air to allow him to breathe. After a long time his hands touched ground. He had been digging in the wrong direction.

He began to expand his room so that he could turn around. It took a long time but eventually he had his feet on the ground and was able to stand. He began digging and moving his feet as though trying to swim in the frozen water. Eventually his hands reached fresh air. When he finally got free he found he could not stand and walk. He had lost his snowshoes and the snow was too deep. He rolled through the snow to the frozen lake and finally found his footing. In struggling through the snow his body heat had melted the snow that was packed around him. It quickly froze again and formed a sheet of ice inside his clothes. He was barely moving when he crawled between the reflector and the cave entrance. He pushed a great pile of wood onto the fire and began to strip himself. Removing the icy clothing helped and gave him enough energy to get into dry ones. The fire scorched the moose hide reflector but warmed the cave. He suffered from chilblains for a week and it took two days just to feel comfortable again but he survived. He left the cave only to replenish his wood supply.

As he sat by the fire looking out over the basin a strange feeling came to him. The setting, with the lake, woods, and cave, reminded him of something, or somewhere, as though he had been in a similar place at one time. He shrugged off the feeling as foolishness, but it persisted.

He considered staying in the basin for a year or two, or even forever. It was a good home. Something kept telling him he needed to move on. He began to feel an urgency to leave as though he were being drawn somewhere. The basin had awakened something in him that he did not understand. He decided that he would leave in the spring as soon as he could find his sword.

Yaweta had lost his sword, spear, snowshoes, and his bow in the avalanche. Most of his arrows had been in his quiver and were broken when the quiver was crushed against his back. He spent some time making new arrows and a new bow. The sword and spear would have to wait until the snow was melted. The winter lasted for some time. More avalanches piled snow in the basin until there was no way to move about. A snow slide above his cave created a great wall of snow around the reflector. It was easily twice as high as the big man was tall. Yaweta was confined to his camp.

When spring arrived the snow in the basin didn't melt until spring was well underway. When the melt happened, the snow went as though a fire had been put against it. The lake was full and the stream became a raging torrent, cutting off the exit. As the trees and grass sprang forth with new life, bluebirds came into the basin. In just a couple of days thousands of them were flying about. Yaweta began calling the place Bluebird Basin.

He searched for his weapons. The spear was sticking straight up and down, half buried in the ground. Yaweta was successful in recovering the weapon but after several days of searching could find no trace of the sword. The weapon that had served him so well and saved his life several times over the years was lost. He experienced a great sorrow because of the loss. It was as though a friend had died. His only remaining link with his origins became the steel knife he carried.

17.
WAR

A few days later he left the basin. It felt strange without the sword bouncing against his leg occasionally. He kept looking to see what was missing out of habit. Using the spear for a walking stick, he went toward the blue mountains to the east. Four braves attacked him the first day. The battle was short and Yaweta won. Four braves had gone to the hereafter. When he camped that night he knew he was being watched so he situated himself in a position that would be easy to defend and easy to sneak away from. He built his campfire next to some rocks and his bed under a tree. The shadows of the tree hid his actions as he made a dummy lump under his bearskin robe and slipped out of the camp. He heard the first native signal his location to his friends.

Yaweta was in no mood to mess with these people. Shortly after he left his bedroll an arrow was shot into it. Three more arrows "killed" the lump he had left behind. If they would strike from secret so would he. Using their own night calls he located each of the braves. Each one silently lost his life until only one was left. Yaweta questioned that one before he bled to death from wounds suffered during the capture. Yaweta learned of the stories about him and how there was a bounty on his life. The promise of great power was a strong motivation for any brave to kill him on sight. These hunters were a part of a larger party camped in a valley just over the next hill. The game they were hunting was him.

Yaweta made a quick run back to Bluebird Basin. He rubbed his clothes with the phosphorus soil and gathered a number of the glowing sticks. These he tied to his arms, legs, and chest. He threw a robe over himself and ran to the hunting party's camp. When the moon went down before dawn the sentries were eliminated and the camp had a frightening surprise. Yaweta stood in the trees at the edge of the clearing holding the campground. He removed the robe and yelled his battle cry at the top of his lungs. As he yelled, he put arrow to bow string and fired. Three arrows killed three braves before he threw the robe over his body and ran back into the trees.

All the Indians saw was a glowing specter and heard the strange yell. They saw their companions fall and the specter disappear. The glowing figure appeared again at a different spot. They heard the yell and three more of their number fell before the figure was gone. Over and over Yaweta pulled the trick. The natives started shooting back but their aim was hasty and Yaweta was just out of the range of their bows. With a much longer range, his longbow could reach its target easily. Yaweta badgered them from various positions, not setting up a pattern. One or two of the braver ones charged him, but were stopped by arrows.

The Indians couldn't understand why their arrows did not hurt him. They knew that at least a few of their arrows had to have been on target but distances are deceiving in the dark. His arrows reached them so they assumed that their arrows were also reaching him. Fear finally took over. They ran off screaming and many dropped their weapons. Yaweta took what he wanted of the spoils and burned the rest.

According to the braves, the man-beast of Bluebird Basin was invincible. It served to keep the tribe away from Yaweta for a while. In the next month he saw warriors a time or two but each time they were running away. It took a whole month for the medicine men to come up with a solution to the problem. They said the man-beast could only be killed in the daylight. When the darkness came he became immortal and would steal their spirits and grow even stronger.

The leaves on the willows and birch trees were turning yellow and the nights were growing colder when he came to the north shore of a very large lake. He had heard about this lake and the legend of a sea serpent in its water. Yaweta had talked to Indians, when he lived with the ones where he had entered the race, who swore they had seen the monster. He was more concerned about Indians than serpents so he picked a campsite in a cave high above the lake. From the high perch he could see the end of the lake to the south but it was a long way off. He kept watch and located two villages along the shore. The nearest one was on the other side of the lake and had some rugged country between him and them so he felt that he might not be bothered. Unless they came by canoe it was not likely they would venture around the lake and up the side of the mountain during the winter.

He was there nearly a month when he saw it. The first snow had come and gone and a time of balmy weather had set in. It was a time of pleasant days and cool nights. He was standing in front of the cave watching the lake. A long brown object was floating just under the surface of the water. It looked like one of the giant cedars until it raised its head. There was a long neck, a smallish head, and a big mouth with jagged teeth. A snort brought a spray of water that, from a distance, looked somewhat like smoke. The thing went back into the water and disappeared in the depths of the lake. As if to verify its existence he saw the monster twice more in the following days.

He hunted his winter meat and processed it. There was plenty of wood on the hillside. Dead trees were scattered about on the ground. They had been knocked over by a landslide, or snow slide, sometime in the past.

Yaweta pulled a number of them to his cave for his winter's fuel. The cave was big enough to put a good stack of wood inside for dry fuel.

He was ready for winter none too soon. Twice during the winter snow slides came down the mountainside. Yaweta's cave was high enough to avoid being blocked in so it didn't worry him. Even if that did happen he had plenty of food and wood to see him through until spring.

Yaweta knew his camp could be seen from the village on the other side of the lake. He could see their smoke so he could see no reason why they had not seen his. Once before the snows came in earnest he knew he had been scouted. The early spring came and he was scouted again. This time he scared the scout away by standing up from a hiding place and yelling when the brave was only a few steps away from him. He saw other braves but they kept their distance. Every now and then he would raise his arms and yell just to keep them away.

The ice was breaking up on the lake and most of the snow was gone from the ground when Yaweta prepared to leave. It was daybreak when he started out of the cave to travel up the river that emptied into the north end of the lake. He thought the water must have come down from the big mountains. They were no longer a far-off blue range. They were close and even higher than Yaweta had imagined. They drew him toward them in a strange way. He felt there was something there he had to see.

Just as he started out he looked down on the lake one last time. He could make out a large number of canoes making their way through the chunks of ice toward him. As they drew closer he could see several braves in each. He felt that it had to be a war party after him or they would have brought fewer men and left more room for their game.

Not really wanting a fight and being so badly outnumbered, he moved off at a trot. It was his hope that when they discovered that he had gone they would return to their homes. He followed the river toward its headwaters moving north and east. That night he chose a campsite on top of a high hill but made no fire. He could see the fires of a large encampment along his back trail.

Cursing the Indians he went to the outskirts of their camp. They had only posted two sentries on the north side of the camp but a distance apart. Yaweta surprised them one by one. When this was done he let loose with his yell and let fly with his arrows. He had killed five in the camp before he retreated. He never knew why but no one tried to attack him.

He slept for a while and two hours later he was back. A couple more sentries died and four more braves in the camp. Each time Yaweta killed a sentry he took the man's arrows. Instead of using up his supply of ammunition it was growing. Two more raids during the night kept the natives on edge. Yaweta was a half-day's travel ahead when they started after him the next morning. He was surprised they followed.

Every night, for three nights, he harassed them. They lost over fifty braves yet there seemed to be more of them every day. Yaweta killed them during the night and more braves joined the war party during the day. He discovered, by their clothing, that there were at least three tribes after him. He took a captive to question him about the reason for the relentless pursuit.

The captive brave was very surprised to discover that Yaweta was human, or at least acted human. The brave didn't think Yaweta looked human but he sure acted that way. Yaweta learned about the predictions and

129

superstitions of the medicine men. He found out that they thought he could only be killed in daylight hours. The tribes were trying to protect themselves from him.

He sent the brave back to his people so he could tell the others that he was not dangerous and would not kill them unless they persisted in their quest against him. The brave tried to tell them but was not believed. Instead, he was dishonored and banished from his tribe for lying.

Yaweta thought it over. For years he had been forced to kill because he was not like the natives of this land. He was a man, a god, and an animal, or a mixture of all three. Now he was being followed and hunted by three different tribes. Something he did not understand had urged him toward these mountains. Yet the tribe from the east of the mountains had joined with the big tribe from the west just to hunt him, even though, traditionally, they were bitter enemies. The third tribe was one that was peaceful to everyone under normal circumstances. He decided to leave them behind and lose them.

Three days later they were a full day behind. He came to a branch in the river. Taking the left arm he went upstream awhile then doubled back floating on a log. The trail he left would confuse them and perhaps they would lose the trail completely. Carefully hiding his tracks he went up the right branch of the river toward the south. If his trail was found it would be after a lot of time was wasted on the false one.

It was not just a matter of walking beside a river. There were places where it was necessary to go up long draws, over a ridge, and down the other side. At the top of one of the ridges Yaweta could look back. It was dusk and time to make camp. He could see the fires from two big parties behind him. By the number and size of the fires he knew the war party had at least doubled. There was no way to tell how many men were after him but it had to be every brave able to carry a bow.

He went down into a draw and made camp. After catching and cooking his meal he rested a couple hours. He traveled for another four hours before stopping to spend the rest of the night. As he lay back waiting for sleep he realized he was traveling through the area as though he knew the trail. He had already figured that it would take four days to reach a certain canyon when he realized that he could not know about a canyon on the trail ahead.

It was almost frightening to realize he subconsciously knew the trail ahead. He knew he had never been there before, but he had a strange feeling of familiarity. He dreamed about a green valley and absolute contentment. He woke up rested and eager for the trail before the horizon turned pink with the first light of day.

The forward scouts found Yaweta's camp and sent a runner back to inform the main party. Thirty of the most fleet of foot and most brave were sent ahead to catch up to and delay their quarry. Three days later Yaweta had just crossed a high plateau and come to the canyon he had expected. A game trail led him straight to a cliff that formed the head of the canyon. A ledge around the face of the cliff made a trail to the other side. He looked back to see the forward scouts coming across the plateau.

As Yaweta made it across the cliff trail the natives ran up to the edge of the canyon. An arrow narrowly missed him as he stepped off the ledge onto the other side. He ran up to the top of the rise out of range of their bows and stopped. As they started across the cliff trail in pursuit, Yaweta stopped them with a barrage of arrows. A few more braves arrived. They tried to reach him with their arrows but could not. Yaweta fought them until he was almost out of ammunition. By dusk most of the scouts were at the bottom of the canyon with arrows in them. When it was dark Yaweta moved on. The scouts followed after the moon came out and they were sure he had left.

He made his way over the top of the ridge and down a long valley arriving back at the river. He automatically turned south, upriver. At this point the river had a cliff for an east bank. The west bank was somewhat level for a while then a low hill met the river. The river itself roared through a narrow cut between the hill and the cliff. From the top of the hill Yaweta saw a lake. The lake was completely walled in except for the south end where the river came between two mountains. The main current followed along the base of the cliff on the east side of the lake.

The two mountains, with the river between them, almost met above the river, and then formed two distinct peaks. The river had made a cut under one of the mountains by erosion and Yaweta could see a valley beyond the mountains. He thought if he could get to it he might escape his pursuers. He stepped into the lake. The bottom was muddy but not overly deep. He wadded across and entered the undercut. The water was shallow and the roof of the cut fairly low so Yaweta was forced to bend down a little. The current in the main part of the stream was too swift and the water too deep so he was forced to hug the side of the overhang. His pursuers topped the ridge and saw him as he ducked and entered the overhang. They started to enter the lake to follow but were stopped by a loud cracking noise. The earth shook and rocks started falling from the mountainsides. When the ground started shaking Yaweta was well under the overhang with a mountain on top of him. He thought he was caught in another earthquake. The mountain from which the undercut was taken gave way with a shower of rocks. One grazed Yaweta's head, knocking him unconscious. The big man fell forward and rolled ending up on his back against the wall. The mountain literally split at an angle and dropped into the stream, cutting it off.

The warriors witnessed the fall of the mountain and scrambled out of the lake. They had seen the mountain fall on Yaweta and knew they were rid of him forever. The fall of the mountain and rocks caused a small tidal wave and then the lake began to drain. After recovering from the surprise they left to report the events to the main body of hunters. The hunting party broke up and each man went his separate way to resume normal activities.

Yaweta did not know how long he had been out. He woke up with a terrible headache and blood in his scalp. He was covered with mud and wet to the skin. He lay still until his mind began to clear and his thoughts were better organized. He was in a tunnel that was formed when the mountain split and slid down. A dim light in both directions showed him the tunnel had two open ends. In his confusion he crawled toward the north end. A large boulder was in front of the entrance, along with many smaller ones. He looked around the boulder to see a lake of mud. The stream, now smaller, still ran along the east wall but the lake was drying fast. Innumerable fish flopped in the mud, dying.

He decided to continue to the valley he had glimpsed earlier. The enemy was still behind him and only the unknown lay ahead. As he reentered the darkness of the tunnel there was a strong feeling he should be remembering something. When he got to the end of the tunnel he was not surprised. It was as though, subconsciously, he fully expected to see what appeared before him.

It was a beautiful valley. Toward the back was a forest of many kinds of trees. In the front was a meadow with animals gratifying themselves on the lush grass. To his left he saw a lake formed because of the dam that had just been created. From the sound that the water made he knew that the stream was only partially blocked and the lake would not flood the valley.

The valley was completely surrounded by mountains and was not really a valley but a very large basin or the crater of an ancient volcano. This entrance looked to be the only way in and out and it was blocked, except for the tunnel. The big man took all this in as an owner looks over his property. A feeling of peace and contentment came over him. He knew there would be no conflict with Indian tribes here, and here he would remain. It only took the first look for him to know his days of exploration were over.

18.
HOME

In a flood of memory he realized he had seen all this before. It was in the fever-induced dream he had years earlier, when he had been bitten by the rattlesnake. He recognized the place and knew that somewhere in the valley there was a cave where he was meant to live. More immediate things demanded his attention for now. Some of the loose debris from the slide had fallen close to the tunnel. From among the rocks Yaweta heard a noise.

The sound was like that of a cat in distress. On investigation he found a mountain lion cub with its tail caught under a rock. He lifted the large rock and expected the cat to scamper away in search of its mother. It didn't go far. Not an arm's length away the fur of a mountain lion could be seen at the edge of a pile of rocks. On clearing them away Yaweta found the cub's mother, crushed by the falling rocks.

He picked up the frightened cub and inspected him. Other than the injury to the tail the animal was not hurt. He determined that it was a male and put him down. He gave the cat a large chunk of dried meat to chew on while he cleared a level place for a camp. He had decided to camp there for a few days and guard the entrance just in case he was followed through the tunnel. The valley made him feel safe but he was not going to take any chances. His dream had indicated safety, but was not clear about whether he had to fight for that tranquility or not.

The lion cub's tail went at a sharp angle, a full hand's width from the tip. Yaweta tried to straighten it but in so doing he hurt the poor kitten too much. He thought that the crooked tail would not cause the cat too much trouble once he got used to it. Yaweta finished uncovering the female mountain lion and skinned it. After burying the carcass he laid the pelt out on the ground so the cub could use it as a comforter.

After building a lean-to from one of his bear robes and starting a fire, he walked out into the meadow to use one of his last three arrows to down a deer. He would recover the arrow and, if it was not badly damaged, reuse it. Three arrows against the mass of people that were following him would not be much of a defense. He decided to try camouflaging the other entrance to the tunnel.

At the other end of the tunnel he surveyed the area carefully. There was no evidence of anyone having been near the entrance, nor could he see anyone around. He rolled some large rocks through the mud to the entrance and then gathered good-sized ones to pile on top of the large ones. As he moved the rocks the mud oozed into the vacant holes, erasing the sign, just as lifting a bite of food out of thick stew fills in the place the food once occupied. Eventually, he had the entrance covered except for a hole big enough for him to crawl through to the other side. After he got back inside he put some more rocks in the hole, completely blocking the entrance. He could only hope it looked natural enough and hid the entrance to the tunnel from the outside. Removing the rocks to gain entry would make enough noise to wake him and give warning.

With the tunnel blocked, and no danger that the light of his fire would be seen from outside the valley, he moved his camp into the entrance of the tunnel. As he did a summer storm sprinkled the area with rain. Sitting there watching the rain and eating his meal, he reflected on the dream. His memory dictated directions. The lake was across the valley from the cave in his dream so the cave

136

he dreamed about must be to his right and along the edge. When the rain stopped a rainbow appeared. It seemed to come from the lake and end at the other edge of the valley.

He could see a large cavern in that direction but it hardly fit the dream's description. He decided he would circle the valley and explore it thoroughly before he settled down. Since the valley in his dream had been real and the events leading to its discovery, he had to assume that the room of jewels and fire were also true. He stood up and stepped out of the shelter. Looking over the area once more he felt that everything was perfect. He turned to the kitten and said, "Well Hook, I guess were stuck with each other".

He stayed in the camp three days then decided it was time to look around. The natives had evidently given up the chase or they would have caused a problem by now. He went out into the meadow and looked back. Curiosity had gotten him interested in why the mountain had fallen. The fault line was evident from where he stood and made him wonder what had kept it from falling sooner. He considered it fate. Along the river he could see the depth of the water. The stream had cut a trench along the foot of a cliff and normally was quite deep but narrow. The melting snow in the mountains had caused the river to be larger than usual and had flooded the little lake on the other side of the tunnel. During dry periods that lake would be quite shallow.

The new lake formed by the mountain sliding down would be long and narrow. The banks were high enough to prevent any serious flooding even when the snows melted in spring. In the center of the lake a waterfall came down from the cliff above. It was not large, but appealing to the eye. Three streams came into the lake near the south end. A lower area of ground

137

caused a marsh where marsh grasses grew. He thought, "Those grasses will make good baskets". Several Moose occupied the marsh, feeding on the grass. The main stream entering the lake came from the mountains directly to the south. The cat, Hook, was right behind him.

He had gone upstream only a little distance when he suddenly stopped and picked up a rock. It was a gold nugget the size of his fist. His first reaction was one of elation at becoming rich. By the standards of his youth this was indeed true. His second reaction was one of questioning its worth in this land where money was unknown. He kept the nugget, tossing it up and catching it again, as he moved along. The stream was rich with nuggets. Once he had spotted the first one he could see them everywhere.

He arrived at the source of the stream, a large spring of hot water at the foot of a mountain, and turned west, traveling along the edge of the valley. Nightfall found him deep in the forest, near the second stream. Again there was a spring of warm water that became the source. A small cave, one of several he had found, provided him with shelter for the night. The next morning he moved on, still rimming the valley. He ran across many animals but not one seemed to be startled by him. It was as though they had never seen a human and did not know they were supposed to be afraid and run away. From this he concluded that the natives had never used the valley for hunting grounds.

In the early afternoon he came across an outcropping of lead ore. He marked the spot in his mind. This might be useful in the future. There were a number of caves around, most of them large enough to accommodate living quarters with plenty of room. After considering each one's advantages and disadvantages, he continued through the forest of old trees. He would decide where he would live after completing his explorations. Some of the trees were big enough to have been a thousand years old. He found a large amount of downed timber and decided he would try to avoid cutting anything down but use the dried wood nature provided. It would be a big job cutting anything without his sword. He sure missed the weapon.

He camped in a grove of slim pine trees for the night. The next day he found the beginnings of the third stream. Like the others, it started with a warm spring near the foot of another mountain and ran almost straight east toward the lake. A line of willows marked its progress along the edge of the forest. The stream acted as a border between the forest and the meadow. Near the stream was the entrance to a cave. It occurred to him that this was about the place where the rainbow had touched down.

The cave's entrance was large enough for him to walk through without stooping but small enough to be a door. It was dark inside so he didn't explore it until after he had made a fire and built a torch for light. The cave was quite large and he saw a second room but didn't get a chance to explore it. There was a loud puff sound as he entered, and blue flame danced around the walls. The second room was suddenly filled with the fire. An eerie glow of blue flame, brighter that the rest came from a large hole in the back of the main room. Yaweta dropped the torch and ran out in fright. He was some distance into the meadow when he stopped to look back.

The door of the cave was bright blue for a moment, and then turned even brighter. A yellow and blue flame shot out in a great ball, carrying dust and whatever else was on the floor of the cave with it. He heard a rumble deep in the ground and the earth shook under his feet. Up on the mountainside he heard a swoosh sound. Looking up, he saw two streaks of flame coming from the ground. One burned a few minutes and went out. The other died down a little, and then got brighter when the first one was extinguished. The cave entrance was dark but Yaweta waited until he was sure there would not be another explosion before going up to the entrance again. There was a draft at the door but inside it was very hot. He decided to wait before trying any farther explorations.

He watched for a while and then continued with his journey around the valley. A few minutes later he was in the cavern he had seen earlier. It was large enough to hold several of the cliff dwellings he has seen long ago. He considered the possibility of constructing such a thing. By nighttime he was back at the tunnel. There was no sign of disturbance so he knew there had been no intruders. Hook seemed relieved to be back.

Just as he had suspected, the only evident way in, or out, of the valley was by the tunnel. With the entrance blocked it was not likely he would be disturbed soon. For the next three days he explored the interior of the valley. There was not a trace of another human being. The valley had berries, roots, and herbs useful both for food and for medicinal purposes. There was plenty of game, and fish in the water. He would lack for nothing.

The fire on the mountain got smaller each day until; finally, it was completely gone. He went back to the cave. It was still warm but not uncomfortable. He made another torch and entered cautiously. The floors had been swept clean by the blast. The main room was quite large and round. The other was somewhat smaller and rectangular in shape. In the main room he found three holes. Two were off the floor and shallow. They would make storage cabinets. The third hole was close to the floor and large enough to walk through by stooping a little. It looked as though it might lead to another room. Before he lit the torch to look around he had seen a dim light at the hole so he was a little apprehensive about farther exploration of its offering.

As he looked around he noticed the smoke from his torch rolling across the top of the cave and disappearing into a small hole in the roof. There was no accumulation as would normally be the case in a cave. The small hole could lead to the outside so he decided to test it. He could not see light through it so he build a small fire and put green grass on the flame, creating a lot of blue smoke. The smoke went into the hole without much buildup inside the cave. He went outside and looked. A column of blue smoke was rising at about the location as one of the flames created during the blast.

He had the perfect home. He could have his warming and cooking fire inside where it would do the most good. There was a spare room for storage of wood and food. The main room had more than enough space to accommodate him and his pet mountain lion, Hook. He could see enough of the entrance to the valley from his door to know if intruders were coming. He decided he had a home. Another part of his vision had come true.

He moved his camp the same day. Yaweta soon relaxed and began enjoying his life. He started making improvements for an extended stay. He hoped he could live in the valley for the rest of his days. Cutting down the slim trees and willows he needed with the knife took a lot of time, but he had an abundance of time. With lengths of wood and wet rawhide he fashioned himself a bed, table, and a chair. His tabletop, mattress, and the seat of the chair were leather.

In so doing he put a little civilization in the wilderness. He hadn't sat in a chair, eaten at a table, or slept on a cot in so many years he had almost forgotten

141

they existed. He built storage shelves and a place to hang meat in the other room of the cave. Doors at the entrance to his home and between the rooms became the final improvements for the time being. At the same time he was making ready for the winter that would eventually come.

Hook became more and more attached to his human friend. He insisted on following Yaweta wherever he went and even slept beside the man. The two wrestled, played catch, and chased each other around as the cat grew to a full-sized mountain lion. Hook was a good companion for Yaweta. His tail never did straighten itself out so the name remained appropriate.

The leaves had turned color and were falling from the willows when Yaweta decided to explore outside the valley. He wanted to know how accessible the area was to marauding Indians. When he got to the other end of the tunnel he found that some of the rocks he had used to block the entrance had fallen and a hole was open to the outside. He pushed more of them out of the way to open a hole large enough to walk through and stepped around the boulder. What once was a small, shallow lake had become a small basin. Grass had started growing and even shoots of a tree or two. The little basin was completely surrounded by a bank with the only easy access beside the stream. The stream had become much smaller and had left a pathway beside it that made it unnecessary to climb over the hill.

He went north, down the stream, until he came to the place where the canyon joined the stream. The cliffs on the east of the stream were consistent enough to discourage access. The stream in the bottom of the canyon joined the one he was following to make a flow of water twice the size of either. The torrent going through the cut formed there made passage impossible.

He wandered up the bottom of the canyon until he reached the bones of the braves he had killed when he first crossed the cliff train without finding a way out of the canyon. Then he turned back to his starting point. He went up his stream a little and camped at a level spot beside the water.

The next morning he went up the valley he had traveled when he was escaping from the natives. Taking his time he took some detours and got to know the land. He arrived at the cliff trail the next day. On the other side of the canyon he saw the smoke of a fire. He approached the edge of the canyon opposite the campsite. Five braves saw him and ran to get their weapons. The canyon was fairly narrow at that point and their arrows could reach him so he began to retreat. Two arrows came across; one nicked his arm and the other narrowly missed.

He had no intention of bothering anyone, but he had been attacked. He used five arrows to dispatch the braves. Others began to show themselves. While some kept him busy six of them ran to the cliff trail. Yelling at the top of his lungs he was able to eliminate a few while moving to a defensive position near the trail. The braves had to go in single file in order to cross. Yaweta waited until they were well on the way before he shot. His first arrow went through one and into the man behind him. As the second man fell, he reached out in desperation and took a third with him. The three braves that remained turned to run. One stepped on a loose rock and lost his footing. He fell into the canyon, joining his companions in death. The other two had almost made it to safety when an arrow took the leader. The last man froze in his tracks, looking back just as Hook caught him. The animal slashed as he went past to the other side. He fell, screaming, to his death.

With most of the Indians dead Yaweta ran across the cliff trail and attacked the remaining braves with his knife. His size, skill, and quickness were too much for the hapless braves. Yaweta kicked one full in the face as he grabbed the wrist of another and pulled him into the charge of the third. They collided and fell. As they recovered he put his knife in the one whom he had kicked. As the other two got back to their feet he took a running jump and kicked both of them over the edge of the canyon. Hook had been successful in running down, and dispatching, two more who tried to get away.

When the battle was over Yaweta picked up the dead men and threw them into the canyon with the others. He salvaged all the skins and arrows and threw everything else into the canyon. His cry of victory could be heard throughout the woods. He went back across the cliff trail and camped.

A small group showed up a day later and looked around. After some time one of them spotted the bodies down in the bottom of the canyon. They began to talk among themselves excitedly, trying to figure out what had happened. It was too far to tell how their tribal members had died. They soon discovered the cause. Yaweta stood at the top of a rise in plain sight and yelled his battle cry. The braves quickly left. He kept his vigil two more days before leaving.

With the additional burden of his loot it was necessary to build a travois for himself and another for Hook. The loads were heavy so he took his time returning. He found little gullies to explore and went up them after leaving the burdens to pick up later. It was a pleasant time for him but one of concern. He had to think of a way to make the natives avoid the area. He spent a lot of time thinking about it, but had no idea other than posting a guard at the cliff trail. He decided to rely on the secrecy of the almost hidden entrance to his valley.

It took three days to get back. He hid his tracks well and was especially careful as he crossed the little basin. He hoped to prevent discovery of his valley. It seemed good to be home and Hook seemed excited as they exited the tunnel. It started snowing as he started toward the cave. It was the first snowfall of the year so it was not very deep, but served as a warning of more to come. Yaweta completed last-minute preparations and settled down for a long winter.

19.
DISCOVERY

As winter progressed he discovered one more advantage to the valley. The mountains around it collected most of the snow. For such a high mountain area the weather was generally quite mild. There was never much snow inside the valley, but outside of the area it got deeper than Yaweta's tall frame. He tried to go through the tunnel once, only to find that the entrance was completely covered with snow. When the occasional blizzard came, it always came suddenly. Yaweta nearly lost his life because of that phenomenon.

It was one of those days when no one in their right mind goes outside. The temperature had dropped to below freezing and a fine, hard snow started falling. The wind was at gale force, howling through the trees. It became impossible to see ahead more than an arm's length. It was a good day for sitting by the fire, not braving the elements. It just happened that Yaweta was not inside. He had been hunting when the snow started and had started back when the wind picked up. He had just left the woods and was crossing the meadow toward home. In a matter of seconds his vision was completely blocked, but he kept going.

Half an hour later he knew he was lost. If he stopped he would freeze to death so he kept moving. Since he had not gotten into the woods or reached a mountainside he knew he was still in the meadow. He turned his back to the wind, letting it push him. This should have guided him straight along to a recognizable landmark. As long as he didn't go in circles he would come to something that he could follow to safety. He knew the valley well enough to get his bearings if he could see or feel something, but in the meadow it was hopeless.

Being in the enclosed area of the valley the wind was blowing in a wide circular motion. He had been walking long enough to think his idea would not work when he found the willows along the creek. He found the frozen stream and thought he should turn to his right but he wanted to make sure. The water was frozen over but under the ice it was running. He broke the ice and checked the direction of flow. Home would be upstream so he turned right and followed carefully. Fighting the blowing snow and the force of the wind took an hour of work but he finally found the spring at the source. He worked his way to the cliff wall and followed it to his front door.

Relieved to be home he stamped the snow from his feet and shook out his coat. The warmth of the cave made him grateful for the extra warmth from the hole in the back. Whatever the fire down there was, it was a blessing. To his surprise Hook was just coming out of the hole. Until now Yaweta had thought the only thing in there was fire. He decided it was time to take a look. The next time Hook went in he would follow.

Getting his big frame through the entrance was not difficult but it was close. Just inside, the passage expanded, giving him more room. A little farther down, the tunnel expanded into a small room but the passage went on down and Hook continued. There was enough space to stand upright and walk along as they proceeded toward the light at the end of a passageway. As he got closer he could see a room at the end.

There were shining stones on the floor and just a glimpse of a pool of water when Yaweta stopped momentarily. "That's interesting", he said and went on. He stepped into the entrance of an underground cavern and stopped dead in his tracks. A thrill of discovery and amazement went through him. It was as though he had stepped into another world. Light filed the room. A single flame shot up from the floor through a crack. The flame was not large, only about waist high and thin, but it was enough to cause a startling effect. Crystals hung from the ceiling in profusion. Many had fallen and were scattered about the floor. Light from the flame reflected in the crystals in every color of the rainbow. The crystals separated the spectrum of light and magnified it, making the room sparkle in brightness. It reminded him of the eggs of the gods he had once discovered. It was like being inside a giant one.

When his eyes adjusted to the light he was able to look around a little more. To the left of center was a pool of water. He went over and put his hand into the water. It was warm. On the bottom of the pool he could see more crystals that had fallen from the roof. He could not help but think of a warm bath for the first time since he was a young boy.

He reached down to pat Hook on the head in thanks for leading him down there. The man and his animal walked around the parameter of the cavern and explored its area. He found several large slabs of loose rock on the uneven floor. There were three levels. The pool was on the lowest level with a flat area around it. There was a little rise and another level then another rise and the larger flat area. Getting to the pool was similar to walking down a couple steps.

On one wall a bright red light caught his eye. The reflection came from the lower section of the wall where the material that composed the rest of the walls was different. All the sides were rock except this area. The material was earthen. There were a large number of red stones imbedded in the wall. He took his knife and pried out a large one. When he held it up to the light he recognized a raw ruby. He took the stone to the pond and washed it. He had found the jeweled room of his vision.

He was anxious to get into the warm water so he stripped down and stepped in. He let out a sigh of relief and relaxed thinking about this latest discovery. The warm water brought back a flood of memories. He fully realized the value of his find. People in the civilized world would kill for less. He could buy off anyone who still harbored any animosities toward him. He could buy property and live the good life. First he would have to be able to get back. He thought about it for a while, letting his imagination run wild. When he envisioned the estate he would have it somehow looked familiar. It was then he realized that his idea of the perfect estate was exactly like the valley.

He started to laugh. He already had everything he could ever want. Hook came over and licked his face as though he understood. Yaweta began to sing and laugh. He splashed water at Hook, who tried to catch it with his mouth. They played that way until Yaweta stepped on a broken crystal. He spent another half hour clearing the bottom of the pool and stacking stones. His jewelers training made him think about using the rubies and crystals to make something. He thought of beads and arrowheads.

When spring came he went to the outcropping of galena. He brought back a good supply to make lead. The fire in the room was blue at the base and became yellow as it got higher. It would be hot enough for melting and heating. He took the raw turquoise he had carried to the crystal room to store it for future use. He carried stones down and used one of the loose slabs of rock to make a table. On the table he had the turquoise, some rubies, crystals, and gold nuggets he had gathered. He was ready

149

to make something if he could find a way to melt the lead.

When he lived with the Cliff Dwellers he had learned about making pottery. He went outside and built an oven in the same manner as he had learned. During the warm weather he made several pottery bowls from the native clay he found. By fall he would be ready to spend most of the winter in his "jewelry shop".

Most of the summer was occupied with providing for winter and making some improvements around his home. He built a house over the spring to keep debris out of it. Freezing was not a problem since the warm water prevented it. He even built an outhouse for those needs, not for privacy, just because it was the "civilized way" and would be warmer when the cold weather hit. He wove baskets from reeds for storage of food and general use. It was a summer of preparation and improvement of the quality of life. He was very satisfied with his life and enjoyed it to the fullest.

When winter finally came Yaweta was ready to make some things. He started by making arrowheads. Crystal made a brittle point that shattered easily, so he experimented with rubies. He found that the gem made a good point and knew it would be in great demand wherever they were traded. After making a good supply he switched to beads. He had some trouble making the hole but the roundness was relatively easy. He made beads of various sizes.

The tempered clay pots worked perfectly for melting lead. He found that he could smash some of the crystals, shattering them into long needles with very sharp points. He made wooden handles to prevent burning his fingers and used the points to place a drop of hot lead exactly where he wished it. By spring he had crystal, ruby, and gold beads filling three of his bowls. He used all the turquoise he had to make more beads. He had shown some Indians how to make points for their arrows out of turquoise so they would not value them as much in the form of beads.

20.
THE SECRET TRAIL

Early in the spring he went to the cliff trail to check things over. There was no sign of intruders but on crossing over to the other side he found a marking at the beginning of the ledge along the face of the cliff. There was a drawing on the side of the cliff. He had seen drawings such as this one time before. He could understand its meaning. It showed a huge hairy creature with fire coming out of its mouth. Several dead braves were depicted at its feet. It was a clear warning to all natives that the area across the cliff trail was off limits. The drawing was very fresh, as were the tracks he found. He decided to investigate farther.

He found the camp of a medicine man and a young brave. He waited until night to approach their campfire. He gave the sign of peace but the two men were very frightened. Yaweta sat down uninvited and indicated his request for them to do likewise. The young man sat back away from the fire while the medicine man came forward. Yaweta could see the fright and smiled. They began to communicate in sign. Yaweta asked the meaning of the drawings. He was told about a large party of braves that had come and been destroyed. No human or animal could do such a thing to so many braves. In a council fire composed of the medicine men of all tribes it had been decided that the area beyond the cliff trail was the territory of a god.

The god had been chased by all of the tribes and had come here as though it knew where it was going. Several natives of good reputation had seen a mountain fall on the god. Yet the god lived. He was seen by a large group of braves and he had warned them not to cross over the canyon trail. The braves attacked the god and tried to invade his territory. He destroyed all but one of them. The sole survivor carried the news to his tribe. Now it would be against tribal law for any man to enter the god's territory. The medicine man asked what else they could do to appease him.

Yaweta quickly decided to go along with the superstition as a means of keeping intruders away. He told the medicine man and his companion that they had done well and were wise. He instructed them to tell of this visit and promised prosperity and victory over their enemies, as long as the taboo was honored. He said he would come to their aid if he was ever needed because of this meeting.

Just as he finished speaking, Hook gave a yowl behind them. With their attention distracted Yaweta seized the opportunity and faded back into the darkness. He heard their exclamations of surprise at his disappearance. He went back across the cliff trail satisfied that he would have no more trouble with the natives of the mountains.

On the way back he was caught in a spring storm. Lightning struck two trees near him and rain poured down. He sought shelter under a large rock beside the trail. As he sat there he witnessed another bolt of lightning strike a cow moose not far away. The moose was dead but the calf beside her was unhurt. It was confused and Yaweta felt sorry for it. He went over and pet the small animal talking to it in a comforting way. Eventually, he coaxed it to the shelter of the rock.

The calf had not yet learned to be afraid. Hook walked up to it and sniffed. They touched their noses together in what Yaweta knew was a sign of peace for animals, just as the raising of the arm, palm out, and was a sign of peace for people. The calf lay down next to the rock with the cat next to it. The man marveled at the friendliness shown between two natural enemies. It reminded him of a story about the lion that lay down with a lamb. His mother had told him about it when he was very young.

The rainstorm lessened to a steady drizzle. He dressed the cow and hung most of the meat from a tree branch with the hide wrapped around it. He carried a front quarter with him when he started back toward his valley. The cat and the moose calf were right behind him all the way. The calf did not hesitate when they reached the tunnel it followed him into the valley. He had a friend whether he wanted it or not; it even followed him right into the cave. Yaweta went out and cut some meadow grass for the animal.

He spent the evening thinking about the possibilities of having a moose for a pet. He decided he would try to keep it and raise it. He might be able to use it for a pack animal and even break it to ride if he did it right. He made two trips back to the site where the cow had been electrocuted before he got all of the meat and the hide home. The task of jerking the meat took several more days.

When the meat was processed he decided to start training his new companion. He began by getting the calf to follow him around and come when he whistled. He fashioned a hackamore from braided leather, then taught the animal to wear it and respond to its commands. Then he began putting small loads on its back and having him carry them. It soon got used to having a strap around his middle to hold the pack. Yaweta found a particular plant the animal liked and rewarded him whenever he did something right. The young bull moose needed a name so Yaweta called it "Lightning" because of the way it came to him. Having the animal inside the cave was a problem that didn't last long. He soon became too big to get through the door.

By the end of summer the moose was half-grown and as tame as the horses back in Erin. It was time to break Lightning to ride. Yaweta did not look forward to the experience. He climbed aboard after a week of jumping up on the animal's back and sliding off. In general, he got his pet ready for the big event by getting him used to it first. When Yaweta sat on Lightning's back, everything went well until he kicked him to get him to move.

The moose stood there trembling as if its feelings were hurt. Yaweta spoke to him gently and slid from his perch. The big man spent a lot of time teaching the moose to respond to the reins and to voice commands. It was not long until Yaweta was riding Lightning all around the valley. Even though there were other moose around, Lightning never seemed to realize he was one of them. There was nothing wild about him although he spent a lot of his free time with the wild ones. All Yaweta had to do was whistle a couple times and Lightning would come running.

During one of his hunting expeditions he saw a big buck deer in a thicket near the south side of the valley. Yaweta knew it was a ticklish shot, but he fired an arrow anyway. The arrow just slightly nicked a limb before it reached the animal. Wounded, the deer ran deeper into the thicket. When Yaweta followed, he discovered a trail leading up a narrow gully. He followed until he found the wounded animal and finished the kill. He carried the deer back to his home on Lightning, but was intrigued by the new trail he had discovered. He was interested in where the trail ended.

He rode Lightning into the thicket the next morning and started up the trail. It was steep and just wide enough for his steed to get through. He traveled for hours. The path seemed to have no end. At one point he was on the side of a huge mountain. Snow was on the ground and the air was thin. He came to the crest of the big mountains. He could see other mountains even bigger to the north and south. To the east he could see smaller mountains and beyond them rolling hills. To the west were more mountains and he thought he could see a prairie.

He went down the other side. One side of the trail dropped into a deep canyon. Above him huge boulders looked as though they would come down and crush him at any time. He went on until he could see that it was possible to travel on through. He had found a second way out of his valley. By this time it was nearly sunset, so he went on down the trail into the foothills to find shelter for the night. The next morning he started back. The trail was easier because he knew the way and what to expect. He considered the discovery interesting. It was not likely anyone would take the treacherous trail but it would serve as an escape route in case of an invasion.

Before he got home he felt the first snow of winter. He was glad to see the valley. Even a light snow in the higher elevations would make the trail impassable. Hook and Lightning seemed just as relieved. His valley was just as he had left it. As he approached his cave he saw two bears at the entrance. He yelled and charged, waving one arm and ready to strike with his spear. The bears ran without any trouble. His door was scratched but secularly latched so there had been no harm. He went to the pool to take a long bath.

During the winter he busied himself making arrowheads, some spear points, and more beads. He began to feel his isolation. He longed to see the wife and son he had left behind. It occurred to him that he just might be able to trade for them. Native custom allowed it and he had something to trade. The arrowheads and beads would be valuable to the Cliff Dwellers.

Spring came and Yaweta began watching the high peaks to be sure the trail was open. It was early summer before he felt it would be safe. He had decided against going out through the tunnel. No matter how careful he was it was certain he would be seen. This might be interpreted as a breach of faith, or it might invite trouble. If the tribes searched enough they might discover his valley. On the plus side he could take Lightning along by going over the top.

21.
A MISSION

The sun had not yet flooded the valley with its warmth when he started up the new trail he had nicknamed the "high trail". Yaweta felt a sense of adventure and anticipation that reminded him of the time many years earlier when he first started to explore the land. The sudden memory of his first son saddened him momentarily. Lightning seemed to understand his master's mood. His pace was faster than usual and his obedience to commands seemed to be immediate. Even Hook seemed more alive and alert than usual. His animals were ready for the new adventure.

The trail was very much as it had been when he explored it the first time. From the top of the mountains, he mapped out a route in his head. He would go east until he met the lower foothills then head south, skirting the mountains. He felt he would come to familiar territory in time and be able to find his destination. He would waste little time and make it to his goal as quickly as possible. There would be time for a short visit with his old friends and his trading. He planned to return with his family as far north as time would permit before the winter snows stopped him. They would have to go back over the high trail during the right time of year or they would never reach the valley.

When he came down the other side and into the foothills he memorized the landmarks. By using the same methods he learned as a sailor he marked the exact angles and elevations. He built a monument to mark the spot and carved the figures in the leather pad he used for a saddle on Lightning. The saddle had the location and a map but only Yaweta could understand the drawings.

They were fortunate not to run across an Indian tribe. With no one living in the area it was not likely he would be followed when he returned home. He hoped it stayed that way. The man, his moose, and his mountain lion, headed southeast, trying to keep the mountain range just to their right. They came to the territory of the Buffalo, the beasts of the plains called "food of life" by most tribes.

A great herd covered the hills and Yaweta's trail went near them. The shaggy headed brutes watched as the man rode toward them on Lightning, with Hook running along beside them. The herd may have been disturbed by the strange procession or by the presence of the mountain lion. Whatever bothered them caused them to stampede as Yaweta and his animals came closer. The ground shook like an earthquake and the sound was as rolling thunder. A great dust cloud rose like smoke from a prairie fire. Hook took after them and didn't return for an hour.

In the next three weeks he saw Indians but always at a distance. Each time he raised his arm, palm out, in the sign of peace. They watched but they never bothered him. Once, a group of braves stood on the side of a hill watching the strange procession. From then on he saw people almost daily. At the end of the third week he came to a large village.

The chief, and the medicine man, met him with the whole village behind them. The chief asked in sign, "Are you Yaweta?" Yaweta answered in the affirmative and a great rejoicing started. When asked to what the tribe owed the visit of the god Yaweta he replied that he was on a journey to the south and would not be stopping. The chief asked him to eat and spend the night.

The medicine man of the village approached Yaweta during the night. Yaweta was sleeping when a

159

small pebble landed next to him. He woke instantly and saw the medicine man invite him to talk. They went to a private place, where they could not be seen or heard. The medicine man had traveled to the northeast and had met other men with hair on their faces. He said the strange tribe, called Mandan, had come from the place where the sun rises. He told these things to Yaweta to let him know that he did not believe Yaweta was a god.

Yaweta told the medicine man he was right. He was of the same people as the Mandan. He told the medicine man that he had not set out to pretend to be a god, but it served to save him a lot of trouble. After a little persuasion and assurances that Yaweta meant no harm to the people the medicine man said that as long as the people believed Yaweta was a god that brought good to the tribe he would not expose him. They ended the conversation as friends. In farther talks Yaweta learned more. Captain Mac and the crew had traveled west to the forks of two rivers and made their homes. They were a strange tribe but were friendly to others and had the respect of other tribes. The tribe was famous for their worship of one God and no others. Other tribes recognized the Great Spirit as the head god but accepted other lesser gods.

The Mandan were raisers of crops and traders but very brave in battle. All but one of the original tribe members was dead but their culture lived on in their children. Some of the original crew was killed during a buffalo stampede. Two or three were killed in battle. The first chief, Captain Mac, grew old and died an honored man. The chief of the tribe, when the medicine man visited them, was the only remaining member of the crew. The medicine man said the chief was nearly as big as Yaweta but he had yellow hair. Yaweta was glad to hear that his friend Sven was still alive. He thought he might go and visit the Mandan tribe one day.

It was several days before Yaweta left his new friends. He spent many hours alone with the medicine man of the village. Since all of their conversations had been in private no one knew what had been said. There was new respect for their medicine man throughout the village. He had talked to a god and when the god left he embraced the medicine man.

Yaweta traveled through rolling hills and forests. There were rivers to cross, lakes to go around, and plains to wander. He met tribes and went past villages several times. They generally fled in fright but occasionally he was greeted with awe and wonder. Most Indians in the southern part of the land had never seen a moose, let alone someone riding one. A pet mountain lion was unheard of. Yaweta himself was enough to cause a stir. The three together were a strange sight indeed. It was three months before he met any hostility.

The general lay of the land had begun to look familiar so Yaweta thought he was getting close to his destination. When he saw smoke signals from the top of a high sandstone pinnacle proclaiming his presence he was sure. He had come to the territory of the Apache tribe. He remembered the meaning of the smoke from his time with the Cliff Dwellers. Later, other signals called together a war party. Smoke from other directions indicated the location of their meeting, how many in each group, and when they would arrive. Yaweta was ready when they started arriving.

The braves came in small groups. As they got close Yaweta killed them from ambush with his longbow. He was taking no chances with that tribe. Only six got through. They gave up the adventure and left to signal for more braves. They discovered dead braves who had been pulled off the trail and hidden under bushes in three different places. Their smoke signal was to call for reinforcements but it never was sent. Yaweta was waiting for them. When the tribe found their warriors they discovered that their foe could understand their smoke. Runners were dispatched to assemble a large war party.

The battle with the war party proved to Yaweta that he was getting close to his destination. The braves were from the particular sect of his old nemesis the tribe that he had fought many years ago. He recognized their dress and the markings on their weapons. A few days later he had found a river that flowed directly south. He thought it was probably the one he had followed north with Sojata when they first explored the area. He followed the river downstream for several miles before coming to one of the enemy tribe's villages.

Most of the braves were gone, so there were only the old, women, and children in the settlement. The moose was bigger than any animal they had ever seen. The man was big and strange. The combination of Hook, Lightning, and Yaweta caused a panic. They ran into the woods and hid as the procession passed through their village without stopping or threatening anyone.

A while later he saw several large groups of braves. He concealed himself and his animals in a thicket and watched as they gathered together in the largest group he had seen in many years. He stayed long enough to learn that it was a war party and he was their intended victim. They talked their strategy over while Yaweta and his companions went on their way. In an effort to avoid conflict he went up a canyon that bordered the west bank of the river. The entrance was wide and strewn with large boulders but it soon became evident that it was a dead end. He was in a box canyon.

By the time he discovered his predicament it was late in the day. The shadows were long and the sun was almost down. When he returned to the mouth of the canyon it was dark. His trail had been discovered and a war camp across the mouth of the canyon, blocking it entirely with sentries. He went back, searching for a way over the cliffs, but found none. The only way out would be through the camp.

Yaweta left Lightning and Hook and worked his way back toward the entrance. The sky was overcast hiding the moon so it was very dark. Guards were posted at close intervals to prevent his escape. He slipped through their lines as rain began to fall. Twice he was almost seen when lightning lit up the sky. Both times the sentries looked straight toward him but their eyes never registered what they were seeing.

Once past the war party he whistled for Lightning. The natives heard the sound and searched for its source but found nothing. The sound of the moose and the cry of the big cat echoed through the canyon. Before long the strange animal with the big horns charged through the native's camp. They could see no sign of Yaweta with the animal so they let him pass. They assumed that the lightning had scared the animal. Having the big man walking instead of riding would be to their advantage. Hook had no trouble sneaking out of the canyon.

By the time they had searched the canyon Yaweta and his animals were far away. He was careful to leave as little sign as possible. What little trace there was of his passing was obliterated by the raid so it was the following day before they found his trail again. The war party was searching for the trail when they were joined by more braves. One of the new men found Yaweta's footprint.

22
THE SECOND SOJATA

The new brave was Big Bear, the son of the chief of all tribes. He was so named because of his size. He was a young brave, not yet fully grown, but taller than any other brave was. His childhood name was Blue Waters because of the color of his eyes. He brought news of the hunt to his father. Instantly the chief knew who was being hunted. He ordered an immediate halt to any effort to harm or interfere with Yaweta in any way. He dispatched Big Bear and ten of his bravest warriors to find the big man and make peace with him. Big Bear and the peace envoy left immediately. The chief remembered the last time the tribes had made war with Yaweta. He didn't want a repeat of the same slaughter.

Yaweta found the place where he had defeated his foes many years ago and followed, by memory, the trail to the Cliff Dwellers. Leaving Lightning at the foot of the cliff, he climbed to the homes. He was greeted by fear and confusion until one of the older braves yelled, "Yaweta you are back!" It was one of his two good friends. Others recognized him, or his name, and welcomed him.

After the initial excitement Yaweta discovered that the old chief was dead. The new chief was the elder of the two young braves who saved his life. Yaweta's wife was killed in the same raid that took the chief. His son had been taken and was believed dead. They gave him back the steel knife he had given the new Sojata. It was found on the body of one of the Apaches after a raid. Over the years the peaceful Cliff Dwellers had been attacked at least twice each year. The tribe had suffered badly. There were less than half of them left and they

164

were about to move away. They planned to join another village farther south and away from the constant raids.

Yaweta traded the beads he had brought for a number of their clay pots and jars. He also obtained eight large urns full of raw turquoise. The beads of ruby, crystal, and gold were a big hit with the natives. They valued them much more highly than the ruby arrowheads and spear points. The few of them that they took would be used for decoration rather than any practical purpose. The load was all he thought Lightning would be able to carry and still be able to travel comfortably.

He stayed with the Cliff Dwellers long enough to know where they would be living and to conduct his business. He was disappointed that he had not succeeded in his original purpose and was anxious to leave. In less than a week he was gone. He planned to get as far out of the territory of the enemy tribe as he could get before snow and cold kept him from traveling. He arrived at the sacred ground where he had lost his first son just as the sun was setting.

He stood beside the grave of the original Sojata and looked down on two large piles of bones. The reflection of the red sunset caused an eerie red glow on the stark white skeletons. It reminded him of the bloodshed. He stayed beside his son's grave. His cries of sorrow could be heard at great distance and lasted throughout the night. Somehow the animals felt his sorrow and their voices joined that of their master. A half hour's journey upriver he was heard by the peace commission.

Big Bear told his companions to wait and proceeded on his own. The other members of the group were glad to wait. Even the bravest of the tribe were struck with fear at the sounds made by Yaweta and the two animals. Big Bear left before sunrise and was not far from the sacred ground when he stopped to wait. Yaweta and his animals moved up the river. His plans were to avoid any contact and still stay as close as possible to his previous route. He had just left the sacred place of his son's grave when he met the first Indian.

Just ahead of him he caught a fleeting movement in the trees. Before he could react, he heard, "Iiieeee Yaweta, father of great warriors, I come in peace". He was shocked to hear the words. Not only was he known whoever spoke the words spoke them in Gaelic, the language of his birth. He called back, "Come forth; let us talk of peace face to face". Big Bear had chosen the place well. There was a clearing between them and two rocks for chairs were about halfway through the clearing.

Yaweta saw a young brave step into the open with his hand raised. The brave was taller than any he had ever seen but still young. He carried his coup stick and nothing else. For a brave so young Yaweta thought he had a large number of the valued marks on his stick. Yaweta stepped forward a few feet. When they were within the range of normal voice the young man spoke again. "I am Big Bear, son of Wolf Track, chief of all Apache tribes." He paused for a moment and then said, in a louder voice, "I am Sojata second son of the god, Yaweta, chief of all Indians everywhere." Yaweta knew that was not true, but recognized the flattery tradition dictated when greeting one of higher authority or rank in the pecking order of life. In this case it was a great way to get his attention.

With great joy Yaweta embraced his lost son. A moment later both men, with their hands on each other's shoulders danced around in abandon. Eventually they sat down to talk. Yaweta had taught his wife his language and she, in turn, taught her son. She had told him all about his heritage and his true father. He knew all the details of the original Sojata's death and the battle that followed.

He was seven summers old when he was taken in a raid and adopted by Chief Wolf Track. Wolf Track was quite old and not able to travel. He had already named Big Bear as his successor. The naming could be challenged and a battle for the title could be fought. The victor would then be chief but the young brave didn't think that would happen. He was very popular in all tribes.

Yaweta told him about his travels and the hardships he had encountered, as well as the victories. He told about the valley and all of its features. He asked Sojata to come there to live. The young man refused, saying it would be better if he stayed where he was. He was very happy and had a young bride with a child on the way.

He invited Yaweta to meet Wolf Track but his father refused, saying there were too many of the tribe who would remember their last encounter and would want revenge for their relatives. Yaweta wanted to get as far north as he could before stopping in order to enter his valley at the right time of the year. By the time they were through talking and getting acquainted, the sun was going down. They made camp.

The ten braves Big Bear left behind became worried and came down the river. They arrived just as the two men were setting up their camp. After introductions, three of them went hunting and brought back a deer. They cooked one of the hindquarters for a feast. The group talked far into the night. In the morning they painted Lightning with symbols and signs. Big Bear gave Yaweta a collar made of beads and porcupine quills as a sign of friendship for all Indians to see.

167

The paintings on Lightning would let anyone know, at a distance, that Yaweta was a friend. Yaweta presented each brave with a ruby arrowhead and his son a necklace, with beads of ruby, crystal, and gold. He gave him several ruby arrowheads and spear points. He made up a gift package for Wolf Track and wrapped it in deer hide. Big Bear sent the ten braves back to Wolf Track with his gift and a message. He would accompany Yaweta until he was out of the territory.

It was a good time for both men. They avoided the villages and traveled at an easy pace, neither one wanting to rush their time together. Almost every time they made camp others would come to share their fire, always bringing food. Several times runners came from Wolf Track to check on them. They learned that the old chief was worried that Big Bear might decide to go with his real father. They were two day's travel out of the tribe's normal territory when the last envoy of five braves arrived. There was a feast of celebration and the next morning Big Bear bid Yaweta a fond farewell.

Three weeks after leaving Sojata behind snow was on the ground and it had become very cold. Yaweta was still on the trail. He came across a small herd of buffalo. Several braves were stalking them but the animals were alert and they were not having much luck. Yaweta was able to help them kill eight of the animals. He helped them carry the meat to their village. The small village had not had food for several days so the meat was most welcome. When the hunting party told of Yaweta's help he became a hero. He decided to help the tribe for a while. He unpacked Lightning and rode into the countryside. They returned with another large supply of meat. The natives divided the meat and each tepee had enough to store some for future use. Yaweta decided to spend the rest of the winter with the tribe.

The first buds of spring were just starting to show when the tribe found he had evaporated into the hills. He had traveled several days when he came across a brave with a crippling ailment. He was not extremely old, but could not travel anymore. His strength was gone. He pleaded with Yaweta to help him.

The brave was called Black Crow. He was on his way to a place called Healing Waters. For many years the Indians of many tribes had used the mineral baths to cure a number of problems. He asked Yaweta to help him get there. The fascination of a pool of water that could cure was enough to cause Yaweta to agree. He stashed Lightning's burden and loaded Black Crow onto the animal.

In three days they were deep in the mountains. They came to an area of steaming hot springs and spouting geysers. It was a mysterious place of strange odors and strange landscapes. A foul smelling yellow stone lined the pools. Gases that smelled like the rocks escaped from the ground. They were startled several times by water spurting out of the ground suddenly. Beside one of the pools they found the place used for healing. Several Indians who had come for the healing were there. Black Crow was interviewed by the resident medicine man and approved for treatment. A few days later he had noticeably improved. Yaweta was no longer needed so he started back to continue his homeward journey.

He didn't get far that first day. Not far from Healing Waters he found a large deposit of a stone that looked like black glass. After an initial investigation he decided it was obsidian, a volcanic glass. His father had some samples of the stone in a glass showcase in the jewelry shop. He had even seen some of it used for settings in rings and broaches. He gathered a pack full of the black rocks and rode back to his stash. He loaded Lightning with his burden and carried the new material on his own back. Hook carried a small pack of his own so all three had an equal burden according to their ability.

Summer was at its peak when Yaweta found the monument he had built. He followed the directions he had memorized and made his way back to the trail he had blazed over the mountains. The trail was very much as it was when he left except for one section. The only pathway led across the face of a mountain. The last time they passed over the trail there had been tracks of various animals but now there were none.

Lightning did not want to cross and it took a lot of coaxing. When he did decide to cross he moved fast. Yaweta had to run to keep from being knocked off the mountainside. Hook shot across ahead of them at a high run. Just as the moose dashed across the mountain trail started sliding. The farther he went, the closer the slide came to catching him. They barely made it to solid ground. Once the other side was reached, Yaweta looked back to see a large section of the trail sliding down into the canyon below. There would be no passage over the top of the mountain in the future.

Much more aware of the safety of the trail he picked their way toward his valley. They crossed several more dangerous places and had to detour around some others. When the man and his animals finally reached the floor of the valley Yaweta felt that a great burden had lifted from his shoulders. His sigh of relief was more for the end of a long journey and coming home than from the pressures caused by the treacherous stretch of trail.

As they crossed to the cave the mood changed from one of relief to one of joy. As soon as they arrived Yaweta had to relieve Lightning and Hook of their packs before the animals ran off. Hook was first and was already chasing around and leaping in the air. Lightning took off for the marsh as soon as he was free of his burden.

Yaweta hauled his new belongings into the cave and sorted out the things he would keep there. He had begun calling the room below, the Room of Lights. The turquoise, obsidian, and large urns were moved to the room along with some of the bowls. Only when he had finished his chores did he allow himself the luxury of a long soak in the warm pool. It was good to be home.

23.
COMPANY

Winter would be coming all too soon so Yaweta busied himself with the preparations. Because time was short and the moose population had grown he took two for his winter's supply of meat. He wondered what Lightning's reaction would be so he made the kills when his pet was not around. The skinning was done and the meat cut into quarters when the man called on his pack animal. By the time the first snows came he had gathered his berries, herbs, and roots, and had a good supply of firewood.

A month later he suddenly got a feeling something was wrong. He checked his supplies and found everything in order. His attention was directed toward the tunnel. If there was danger it would likely come from there but he found nothing amiss. He decided it was only his imagination.

A few days later he was working on a ruby ring when his thoughts took him to the area outside the valley. The territory from the cliff trail to the valley was supposed to be his and no one was allowed to enter. He decided it might pay to take a look. Lightning gave him a ride to the tunnel. He had barely exited the tunnel when he saw movement.

He saw a young boy carrying a rabbit. The brave was just going over the small hill at the north end of the basin. He looked like a young brave, but was dressed differently than most Indians he had seen. As Yaweta followed, he detected the faint odor of smoke. He saw the brave again as he exited the basin. He was just disappearing into the woods downstream.

Silently, and with great caution, Yaweta followed. He found the camp at the level spot where he had once camped. Some of the trees had been cut to use for poles for the tepee standing in the clearing. From the discoloration of the stumps and other signs he estimated that the camp was set up some two or three months after he had left the valley for his trip south. The native was near the fire skinning the rabbit in preparation to cook a meal.

Very slowly an old man and woman came out of the tepee. One rabbit would not make much of a meal for three people and these looked as though it had been some time since they had eaten properly. The way the three tore at the food when it was barely cooked proved that the assumption was true. Their moccasins were worn out and rabbit furs were tied on their feet. The furs they wore for warmth were old and falling apart. The young brave turned around while cleaning up after the old couple finished eating. Yaweta got a good look at the hunter. It was not a young brave, but a full-grown maiden and a very beautiful one at that.

At the sight of the young girl Yaweta felt a strange emotion. He interpreted it as feeling sorry for their plight. The old man and woman were in bad shape. They were obviously in poor health and shook with the cold. The girl was doing everything for them. Yaweta could see that she was providing for them as best she could and was sacrificing herself for their well-being. He noticed that she took only a front leg of the rabbit and gave the rest to them. Yaweta came closer until he was beside the tepee. He could see the bow and arrows. The bow was small. It was the kind used by children to practice hunting skills. It was not strong enough to kill game big enough to supply the three with food. There was only one arrow in the quiver and it had been used several times. The feathers were torn making it so it would not fly true. The old woman got up slowly and shuffled back toward the tepee so Yaweta left.

An hour later the girl heard a knocking sound close to their camp. It sounded as though someone were pounding a tree with a stick. Taking her bow and her last arrow, she went to investigate. She found a deer hanging in a tree and the tracks of a giant man. They were the largest footprints she had ever seen. The venison had been quartered to make it easy for her to carry. The hide was folded and lay to one side. She took one of the quarters and the hide and went back to the fire. When she got back she found that her quiver was full of arrows. Each arrow had a ruby point.

When she finished cooking the meat she carried food into the tepee for the old couple and then sat by the fire to keep watch and enjoy a good meal. As she sat down she noticed that her bow had been replaced with a new one. Cutting a large portion of the venison, she put it on a clean piece of bark and set it on a rock within the light of the fire. She walked back to her fire and turned to start watching to see if her benefactor would come for his meal. When she turned around the meat was gone.

After a few days the old couple seemed to have gained a little more strength so she decided to go hunting before her food supply was depleted. She walked around but found no game and was returning home when she saw Yaweta's tracks. She followed until she saw the man making them. She watched from her hiding place while the big man dressed out a deer and hung it in a tree. He quartered the deer and folded the hide just as he had done the first time. When he finished the big man looked straight at her concealment and raised his arm in the sign of peace.

She didn't know what she had seen at first. It had to be a man because of its actions but it was a very large and different man. She made no sound when she followed his trail and was well concealed while watching. Yet he knew exactly where she was hiding. She accepted the presumption that he was of a strange tribe. She returned his peace sign and approached him.

Yaweta stood in plain sight, working with the deer and hanging it for the girl's use. He wanted her to see him from a distance so she would get used to his unique appearance. She walked up to him boldly. He saw no fear in her eyes as she approached. Her body language said she was apprehensive but not afraid. Yaweta put all four quarters of the deer on his back and picked up the hide. Without a word the two of them walked toward the camp. When they arrived he hung the meat from the branch of a nearby tree.

The girl lost interest in Yaweta immediately. The old man never noticed the big man. There were other problems. The old woman had left the tepee and was lying on the ground with her head and shoulders in the old man's lap. He was chanting a death song when Yaweta checked her over. Her pulse was weak but steady and she was running a fever. The old man was sweating even though it was freezing cold. In sign Yaweta told the girl that the only chance the old couple had to live was for him to take them all to his home.

At first the old man refused, saying it was the will of the Great Spirit that they should die. His eyes grew wide as it finally registered that he was not talking to an ordinary man. Yaweta took advantage of the initial amazement and told the old man he had been sent by the Great Spirit to help them. In so saying he slyly winked at the girl. The wink, or some chemistry, formed a bond between the girl and the man. She trusted the strange man but knew not why. Once they all agreed to go with him he told them he would have to cover their eyes because it was a secret place. The girl thought it was a way to get the old man to go along so she agreed.

He covered their eyes with pieces of soft deer hide, picked up his patient, and had the other two hold on to him. He did what he could to confuse their sense of direction and led them through the tunnel. He whistled for Lightning and loaded them on his back. Once at the cave he waited until they were inside before removing the blindfolds. They had never ridden on an animal and had no idea of what had happened. All they knew was that they had been carried and had arrived at a nice warm cave.

Yaweta laid the old woman down on his own bed and insisted the old man lie down with her. He said it was to comfort her but Yaweta knew the old man was nearly as sick as his wife was. He covered them with furs and made them comfortable. He made a stew of meat, roots, and herbs with one of the larger clay pots. While the stew was cooking he made a tea of medicinal herbs for the old couple. The girl ate some of the stew while the other two guests had broth. At Yaweta's insistence she also drank the tea. He made pallets for the girl and himself and insisted that everyone rest. There was little talking other than was necessary. There would be plenty of time for that after the fevers broke.

The next day, after instructing the girl as to the care of the old couple Yaweta went back to their camp. He removed all signs of the camp. Though worn the hides that made the tepee and their bedding were needed for their comfort. All their belongings were carried through the tunnel and loaded on lightning. The campground was as though it had never been. As he arrived at the cave the girl came out the door. The expression on her face when she saw the moose being used as a pack animal was something to see. It was not the last of her surprises.

Yaweta unloaded Lightning and carried everything inside. He moved the old couple to thick, comfortable pads made of the skins from the tepee. He made a similar pad for the girl with other skins and furs. She asked why he had brought everything so he told her they would be spending the rest of the winter with him. The patients were feeling much better and were able to sit up to eat some of the stew.

Yaweta sat in the back of the cave near the entrance to the room of lights while they were eating. Hook came out of the passage and lay down beside his master. Yaweta began taking meat out of his bowl and feeding the cat. They all ate in silence each dwelling on personal thoughts. Hook had been there for several minutes when Yaweta heard a gasp. He looked at the girl. She had stood and was looking at the big cat with her mouth open. It looked as though she was about to faint when Yaweta casually reached over and pet the animal's head and smiled. The girl sat down again slowly shaking her head.

It was several days and yet they had not talked. After the evening meal the old man indicated, in sign, that they were well enough for some conversation. The old woman had regained her color and the light was back in her eyes. Yaweta had wanted to know some things about them so he decided it was time to get acquainted. He asked their names. The old man spoke for the family.

24.
THE LIVING DEAD

He had been called Big Tree, but his name had been taken from him and now he was without one. His wife used to be Morning Star, but she, also, lost her name. The girl was their daughter and was called White Bird.

The old man said, "I think you must be the god Yaweta, the Protector of the People". When Yaweta nodded the old man smiled. He had made the assumption from the legends he had heard and the description he been told by a native who claimed to have seen the god, Yaweta. He asked if they had died and were now in the afterlife.

Yaweta told them all about himself and how he had made friends with the two animals. He made it clear that he was just a man and not a god but the old man never quite believed him. Yaweta told of his beginnings and how he got the name. He went through his life history in a way he thought they would understand. By the time he was through speaking the hour was late. As everyone was preparing for bed White Bird came over to him and said, "I'm glad you are not a god". Then she ran to her bed. The next day when the daily chores were done, and after a good meal, they talked again.

The family came from a tribe east of the big mountains. They lived mostly in the foothills, but each year they made a trip to the prairie to hunt the great herds. Their life was very similar to the tribe that gave Yaweta his name. They were called The Real People and the nation had many tribes. Big Tree had been chief of one. He had lost his office through treachery.

In his younger years Big Tree had been well respected and always first in battle. Whenever his band was attacked he killed many enemies and served well as their leader. His band was a small tribe that was part of a big nation, made up of hundreds of small tribes. The nation as a whole never purposefully went out of their way to attack their neighbors, but any trespass was met with immediate and violent action. The nation never allowed incursions into their hunting grounds without permission. Likewise, they respected the territory of other nations.

They held a vast territory, stretching from the big mountains in the west to the prairies of the east. The whole nation gathered in the plains once each year to hunt the great herds for winter meat and robes. Each tribe was independent from the rest of the nation but when one tribe was invaded the whole nation would come to their aid.

As the years passed few battles were fought. The young men began to yearn for adventure but the chief kept them in check. One young man demonstrated great skill in the use of weapons and had become a very successful hunter. His popularity made him the leader of the young braves in age his group.

When White Bird had became of age he brought gifts for her hand in marriage. Chief Big Tree accepted the gifts because he was fond of the younger brave and he would be a good provider. White Bird was not happy about the choice. She sensed something that others missed. Although the bride had no choice as to whom she would marry she was the one to set the date. White Bird had kept putting the wedding day off. He had not pressed her because he was more interested in adventure. Big Bear never knew of his dark side at the time. The young brave become a hero in one of the rare battles. The recognition gave him a thirst for war.

His popularity was such that he became the war chief after the old one died mysteriously. Soon thereafter he led a band of his friends into the territory of the nation to the north. It was against all laws of the tribe, and of the nation, but they went ahead in a deliberate attempt to start a war. They wiped out one village and returned. They were victorious over old men and children because the young men had been away. When the braves of that tribe returned to their village they followed the raiders.

Since the raid was a violation of tribal custom and law the chief and many of the tribe refused to take part in the victory celebration and demanded the young men take their celebration elsewhere. The celebrants were attacked in the height of the festivities. Before the avenging natives were driven off half of the celebrants were dead. The war chief was wounded just enough to make him angry.

He was a man with a persuasive tongue. By the time the survivors had returned to the village they had decided to replace the chief of the tribe with the young war chief. In an eloquent speech of innuendo and outright lies Big Tree was blamed for everything. In the end Big Tree was banned from the tribe. He and his wife were to be considered as dead. Their only relative, their daughter, was ordered to take the "bodies" into the forest and tend to the burial. She was to return in three suns and honor her commitment to marry the new chief.

In the tradition of The Real People the dead had no names. Therefore Big Bear and his wife had their names taken from them. It was forbidden to speak the names of the dead so there was no need for an identity. They would be given new names in the afterlife. The names they had on earth could then be used over again.

White Bird knew when they left their village that she could not place her parents on a burial platform to die of starvation. She knew she was expected to build the platforms and tie her parents down. The short time allotted her would not allow her to wait and remove the bonds. She was not only expected to kill her own parents she was expected to shame them. Even if the accusations had been just she would not be able to fulfill such a horrendous duty.

She led her parents deep into the woods toward the setting sun, feeling only hate for the deceitful man she was supposed to marry. She could tell they were being followed but she doubled back to make sure. She left the old couple in a little ravine and crept around to come up behind the watchers. The observers were the three closest friends of the new chief. It was their mission to see that she fulfilled her duty and returned. She heard them talking about catching up in the morning and forcing the issue.

When she told her father what she had learned they decided to leave immediately and travel north during the night. They hid their trail well and managed to get into the territory of the northern nation. Those who followed were less careful and were killed. The northern tribe thought the three men were scouts for another incursion into their lands. The fugitive family was hiding in the brush when they saw a war party heading south to retaliate. A real war was starting.

They camped here and there for seven month before they found their way over the mountains and up a river that flowed from the south. They came to the cliff trail. Their clothing was worn and they were tired from hiding all the time. Their food consisted of fish, small game for meat, roots, and berries. Their only weapon was the child's bow and arrows White Bird had been permitted to carry for her own survival.

Upon seeing the taboo signs at the beginning of the cliff trail they decided to risk entering the sacred territory. The old man made a remark about suspecting that the creature whose likeness was painted on the rocks was the Giant Protector of the People. He knew that if he was right no harm would come to them. By then they were free of their own tribe but needed to hide from the tribes of the northern nation.

They crossed the cliff trail and found their way down to the stream. When they arrived at the stream they turned downstream and found a good level place to set up their new home. It was midsummer when they arrived. The women set up the camp while the old man hunted. At his age he no longer had the strength in his arms to pull the string of a full sized bow so he made do with the child's weapon. He was able to provide sufficient meat and fish for the winter. The women gathered roots and berries. They sewed together rabbit furs for warm bedding. They had not been permitted such things when they were sent away. It was cold and they ran short of food but they survived. When spring came the old man began hunting and fishing in earnest. With all of them working, by the time the first snows fell, there was plenty of food. There was leather to make moccasins and fur for clothes during the winter months. Everything was looking good.

The old woman came down with congestion in her chest that would not go away. As it became worse she started running a fever and became weak. The old man was almost as sick so he could not do the chores required for daily life. The whole burden of camp duties fell on the shoulders of White Bird. When spring arrived the old couple got a little better but they were still weak. White

Bird worked hard, catching fish, rabbits, and quail. She was able to kill two deer with the small bow, but it cost precious arrows. They were ill prepared for the cold weather and deep snows of winter. Her mother and father began to get worse as the weather turned cold and damp. To make matters worse they had a visitor during the night.

Their store of food was hung in a tree to keep it away from animals, but a grizzly bear came into the camp during the night. What he did not eat, he desecrated. Their entire food supply was ruined. They were actually fortunate he got the food. He could have been after them just as easily. By then the snow was deep enough that snares were not effective for catching small game and the stream was heavily frozen so fishing was out of the question. White Bird broke two of their last three arrows by shooting rabbits. The arrows went straight through and broke on rocks. She salvaged the points, but needed to make new shafts. The scarcity of game reduced them to one meager meal a day. The old couple was not getting any better. They hadn't had a meal in three days when White Bird killed the rabbit and Yaweta found them.

25.
THE MARRIAGE

While they signed back and forth each spoke in their own tongue. Yaweta began to understand their dialect and they began to understand his words. Yaweta preferred to speak Gaelic because it was the true language of his native land. He knew and spoke English and several Indian languages but Gaelic was his personal choice. It would not be long until sign language would not be needed. In the course of time they would all speak Gaelic.

Since the old man and woman had no names and didn't want their old ones back Yaweta asked what he should call them. With a twinkle in his eye the old man said, "How about Mom and Dad?" Both people of the older generation had seen the way the two younger people had looked at one another. From that time they were called by those names. The girl wanted a new name too. She was just as dead to her old life as her parents. If her parents were supposed to be dead, so was she. She was starting a new life and a new heritage. Little did she know how different her new life would become. She left the choice of a name to Yaweta. A few days after the conversation, Yaweta went hunting. Just after leaving the meadow and entering the woods near the lake he saw a fox running through the snow. It was then he decided on the new name for the girl. She would be called, Alzora, which meant Little Fox. He hurried home to tell her of his decision. As he came up to the cave he found the girl outside of the entrance, without her clothes, rubbing herself with snow. She was taking a snow bath in the custom of her former people. She had not expected Yaweta back so soon so she had taken the opportunity to clean herself. She covered her body quickly and ran into the cave. When Yaweta came in she was dressed but totally embarrassed.

That night, after the evening meal, Yaweta asked the family to discuss an important matter. He asked if they would like to live in the valley forever. He cautioned them that they would never be able to leave but promised their continued happiness. The old man said they had already discussed the possibility but were afraid to ask. Yaweta decided it was best to be honest with them. He said the valley was secret and had many more secrets than its existence. He promised to show them everything. That business being concluded, he said, "There is one other thing". He went outside and brought in a new bow and a quiver full of arrows. He presented them to the old man and asked, "I would like Alzora to be my wife, but only if she is agreeable. This will not affect your decision to stay in the valley in any way".

Alzora got up from the bed where she was sitting and came over to Yaweta. She put her hand on his arm and said, "If my father agrees I would like very much to be your woman." The bargain was made and Alzora was given to Yaweta. The next week would be the feast, with dancing and a marriage ceremony. Preparations for the wedding put the small group in a festive mood.

Yaweta secretly carried a number of furs down to the room of lights and made a soft bed. He made a gift for his bride and placed it on the soft bed. It was a collar of white doeskin with five rows of beads radiating out from a single large ruby mounted in gold. Each row of beads alternated colors, one each of gold, ruby, crystal, obsidian, and turquoise. A supply of food and fresh water to last three days completed his preparations.

Dad suggested that he and his wife move to another cave for a while, so Yaweta and his bride could be alone. Yaweta told him he would take his bride to a special place he himself had prepared.

Mom secreted herself in the storeroom to make a wedding garment of white doeskin. The fittings were done when Yaweta was away so he would not see the garment. The dress was almost finished when Yaweta handed Mom a leather pouch filled with beads. Mom put the beads to good use. When Alzora put on her wedding dress before the ceremonial party it was decorated with gold, red, black, and green beads.

The night of the festivities the young couple was the guests of honor, Alzora in her dress and Yaweta in his finest buckskins. The older couple served a grand feast. Then the old man played a drum he had made while the others danced. The celebration lasted until very early in the morning. It became time for the main event when the new day was dawning.

The wedding ceremony was simple. Dad took Alzora's hand and made a cut in the fatty tissue at the heel of her palm. A similar cut in the groom's hand completed the preparation. The two hands were then bound together with leather so that the wounds met. Dad then held their hands in his and said, "The blood of one is now the blood of the other. These two have now become one person. The bride price has been paid and this, my daughter, has agreed. She is the flesh of her husband and he is her flesh. From this time they will act as one, think as one, and be one. Each of you must treat the other well and you shall both be comforted throughout your days." With this the ceremony was over. "Dad" and "Mom" were now appropriate names for the old man and old woman.

Yaweta led his bride through the tunnel and to the room of lights. Her cry of delight, upon seeing the room, could be heard by her parents and pleased Yaweta. After she recovered from the thrill of the room he presented her with the collar and received another squeal of delight as she jumped into his arms. He swung her around and let loose with a shout that sounded much like his battle cry.

After a while he led her over to the pool and removed her wedding dress and his own clothing. They embraced for a while before he led her into the pool. When her foot touched the water she jerked back in surprise and then stepped in with another squeal. They bathed each other for a long time before anxiously retiring to the marriage bed.

Mom and Dad heard the squeals and the shout of joy. They looked at each other knowingly and smiled. Reluctantly, four days later, the newlyweds ended their honeymoon and went up the passage to begin their life together.

Alzora couldn't wait to show her mother the collar and tell her parents about the room of lights. They led the older couple down the passage to visit the room. Yaweta showed them where he had been working and the things he had made. They sat and listened as he told all about the discovery of the cave, the explosion, and the finding of the room.

He told them about the vision he had experienced in a fever-induced dream, many years earlier, which foretold everything. The newlyweds spent their nights in the room of lights for the rest of the winter. By spring Alzora was with child.

Yaweta started a school. Almost every night he taught his new family how to speak, write, and read Gaelic. He was starting a new tribe and wanted one with education as well as intelligence. The Indians did not have a written language so he had to start from the beginning. The only things they had ever read were the signs of the trail and seasons. They were good students and learned rapidly. When the Chinook winds came and nature came to life after her winter's sleep everyone was becoming quite literate.

At Dad's insistence the older couple moved to a cave not far away. The men made the necessary improvements and moved the older couple's belongings. They built a small room on the front of the cave. It contained a strong door on one side and left enough room for a fire. A hole in the top let smoke escape. In this manner the older couple could heat their home.

The time for his bride to get to know Lightning came with spring. Hook had already gotten to know everyone and had taken a particular interest in Alzora. It was not always so. He had been offended when Mom and Dad kept him out of the room of lights during the honeymoon and blamed Alzora. It was as though he was jealous at first but Yaweta's love for her affected the cat. He soon followed her everywhere she went as though he were her protector.

The first time Yaweta put Alzora on Lightning's back she almost fainted with fear. Yaweta acted surprised and reminded her that she had ridden the animal when he first brought her into the valley. She was not impressed. She had seen Lightning used as a pack animal but to ride an animal was completely out of the question. Before long she wanted to ride everywhere. The family accepted the concept of riding an animal as just another of the strange things about Yaweta.

The summer was spent preparing for winter while Yaweta showed everyone all the features of the valley. The more they saw of the land the more they were happy about their decision to stay. Yaweta's territory included the area south of the cliff trail so he took them through the tunnel and went through that area as well. This was the area where he took most of his meat. The valley animals were reserved for the future and were only killed to thin the heard. Even then he only killed them during the winter months. He practiced a strict stock management program with vigor.

26.
THE REDSTONE NATION

One cold winter morning Yaweta woke to a new sound. He heard a baby crying. During the night Alzora had slipped out of bed, went outside so as not to disturb her husband, and gave birth to a boy. In typical native fashion she took care of everything herself. After cleaning the baby with snow she carried him inside as he sucked a nipple for his first nourishment. It was several minutes before his little cry woke his father.

Yaweta named his son, "Telia". When he became a brave he would be given another name, which he would earn. It was a good thing they had plenty of provisions and little need to go hunting. Yaweta spent most of his time with Telia while Alzora made baby clothes and did the other things necessary to keep the child healthy. Mom and Dad were typical doting grandparents. The women helped each other with chores while the men spoiled the child.

The grandparents were on one of their daily visits when a great storm hit the valley. For the first time since Yaweta first discovered the valley snow fell for three days. By the time the weather cleared the small tribe was confined to their home. It was a full two weeks before Yaweta could make the trip over to the grandparent's home, on snowshoes, to get some of their things. Lightning was deep in the forest foraging for food. Even the big animal would have trouble in the deep snow. It was two months before Yaweta would let the older couple return to their own cave.

During this time they held a family conference. Dad and Yaweta started discussing the new tribe that had been started. When the baby was sleeping the women joined the conversation. It was a session of dreams and speculation but not one without foundation. Yaweta's "tribe" was across a great ocean and he was an outcast. The others were no longer a part of their own people.

Even if they returned to their old home they would be treated as though they were not there. The tribe considered them dead. They realized they were all outcasts and had no existence as a part of any nation. The idea of a new tribe was more than a dream. If their descendants were to have any identity, it was a necessity.

With Yaweta's guidance they all agreed. Since there was no Indian word for ruby and they would have to have a name other tribes would know, they decided the tribe would be known as the, "Redstone", tribe. Their trademark would be the ruby-tipped arrows and spears. They would be a people of crafts, making arrows, spears, and beads. These would be traded to other tribes. The arrows and spears would have points made from agate, flint, or other material, but never ruby. The ruby point would be used by the Redstone and no one else.

The tribe would be unique in several ways. They would have but one God. The Great Spirit would be their only deity. The minor gods of other tribes were not real. Had not Yaweta been called a god several times? Was he, even now, considered one by the tribe living downriver? All Indians believed in the Great Spirit but none believed they could talk directly to him. Yaweta told his followers about the Son of God who died, and was raised up from the grave. The Son became their mediator between them and the Great Spirit.

The language of the tribe would be Gaelic. There would be a school where the children would learn to read and write. They would be taught the language of other tribes and their customs. The history of the Redstone; their, religion, medicine, and laws would be taught.

191

When Yaweta was a young boy he had gotten a rudimentary education in martial arts and had improved on it by learning the hard way - fighting in the streets. Self-defense and the use of weapons were to be an integral part of the school. The Redstone would be peaceful, but the most fierce of all when necessary. There would be no better fighters.

There would be a written law. Even the chief would be subject to the law and any breach would be met with certain punishment, generally death. The law Yaweta would eventually write down, on buckskins, was similar to the ten commandments of the Christian Bible. The chief would be both the spiritual and governmental head of the tribe. At first Yaweta would have the final say in all disputes and all matters of law. Eventually that would be changed to a council of seven with Yaweta as chairman. A vote of the people would be binding on the tribal leader and the council.

The Redstone would have a chief but he would not be called the chief. The office would be passed to the eldest living son of Yaweta and Alzora. The name Yaweta would no longer be only a name, but both a title and a name. Yaweta became the first "Yaweta" of the tribe. As the name implies, the Yaweta would be the Protector of the people. A ceremony would mark the transfer of the title at the death, or designation, of the old Yaweta.

There would not be a war chief, or the counting of coups. A young man would become a brave by scholastic ability and demonstrated skill. There would be no torture tests, as was the manner of many tribes. If the brave had enough ability in stealth, intelligence, and fighting, there would be little need to endure torture.

Yaweta felt that a brave would have more incentive to get out of bad situations if he had a little fear of being tortured. The first Sojata had never been through the rites of becoming a brave and had never had to endure torture to prove his manhood. Yet he never cried out when the Apache tribe did their best to make him scream for mercy. The same quality of character would be taught to Yaweta's descendants.

After the brainstorming session, Yaweta spent many hours thinking about his Tribe. Once spring arrived he was ready. He went to an isolated place to write the laws, history, and all the things they had decided. Once started he thought of many things they had not previously discussed. They had proposed broad principals and goals. Now he needed to contemplate all the ramifications and complete the details.

The place where he had his retreat was a level place on the side of the mountain near the tunnel. He was standing there, watching the sunset and thinking over a problem. The forest was blue-green because of the light and the needles of the trees. To the left, the lake showed crystal clear. In front of him was the meadow. It took a reddish hue as the sunset reflected in the moisture on the grass. The meadow looked as though it were on fire. He took a stick and absent mindfully drew a design in the dirt at his feet. It was somewhat like a wheel with three spokes. In the center he drew a circle.

By the time his business at the retreat was finished he had written everything on buckskin scrolls. He carried the bundles back to the others. They studied the documents until they were familiar with their contents. Afterward, he placed them in the room of lights for safekeeping. They would become the textbooks from which children would be taught about the tribe and its laws.

Yaweta had forgotten about the image he drew in the dirt. Each night, for three nights, he saw the image in

193

his dreams. Each time it was more vivid and each time he felt as though it were important to the tribe. He felt compelled to complete it. He put the design on a large piece of buckskin, sewing gold beads for the lines. He sewed crystal beads, representing the water of the lake, in the left triangle, turquoise beads in the right triangle represented the forest, and ruby beads on the bottom triangle for fire. It was just as he had seen it from his retreat, and in his dreams. In the center was a large gold nugget, representing the sun. His feelings led him to make a necklace of gold beads with one large polished nugget in the middle of the string. This would be worn by the Yaweta of the tribe.

He called his family together, told the story of how the inspiration for the symbol and necklace had come to him, and presented it to them. He told them every Redstone Indian should wear the symbol. The women went right to work, sewing the emblem on the clothing. The old man composed a song pledging allegiance to the symbol and extolling the virtues of the Redstone Tribe.   The tribe had a flag, and a national anthem, just as nations in the old world. It was something other tribes would recognize from a long distance. As the Redstone Indians became known, the flag would be respected by anyone who saw it. He went out to the cliff trail and placed the symbol on the face of the cliff beside the drawing that the medicine man had placed there. This marked the boundary of his territory.

27.
JUSTICE

Two years passed. Yaweta needed to get some more turquoise and some obsidian. He had never been able to equal the skill of the Cliff Dwellers when making bowls and urns. He thought it would be nice to have some more of their good pottery. Alzora had delivered her second baby boy in the fall and was strong again. Mom was a big help with the chores and the two babies. Dad was strong and could handle the hunting and fishing. There was no reason not to make the journey.

It was early spring when Yaweta went through the tunnel. He carried a good supply of ruby, gold, obsidian, and crystal beads with him. Jewelry made of combinations of gold and rubies, or other stones, completed his trade goods. He hoped to avoid contact with other tribes until he was well out of the territory. This was not to happen.

He crossed over the cliff trail and went down the river to where he had first turned up the south fork. He made his way east from that point. He went over a high mountain pass and entered the foothills. Through carelessness, being out of practice, or just plain dumb luck, he walked right up to a village. By the time he realized what he had done he was surrounded. He decided to be peaceful.

An old medicine man came rushing toward him. It was the one with whom he had made the agreement at the cliff trail. The tribe still believed he was one of their gods and they greeted him in that way. Both the old medicine man and the younger apprentice walked ahead proclaiming Yaweta's identity and telling the people to welcome him. They assumed he was there to help them with their war. The whole nation had been drawn into a war with the nation to the south. Hundreds of tribes were involved.

Yaweta sat down with the chief of the nation, the various chiefs of the tribes, medicine men, and war chiefs, to discuss battle plans. They were preparing for a big battle with the nation to their south, in hopes of ending a war that had lasted several years. After listening to their plans Yaweta asked how the war started. He was told about a vicious sneak attack that had started everything. He asked them to delay their plans so he could bring an end to the war without farther hostilities.

He told them a story about an ambitious war chief who had betrayed a peaceful people. The war chief had not only offended the northern tribes but had betrayed his own chief and his own tribe. His treachery was not known to his nation's leaders. Yaweta would go to the camp of the southern nation and bring back the offender for punishment. Then both sides could meet and straighten out their differences in a more peaceful manner. There was ready agreement, but they would only wait for three suns.

Scouts showed him where a like assembly of the southern nation was being held. He left the scouts to wait until he returned and walked into the meeting. He was able to slip by their guards and seemed to just appear. These Indians had never seen him but the old men had heard tales about him. He walked up to the fire; arms raised, and surprised them all by calling out in their own tongue.

"I am Yaweta, Giant Protector of the People. I have come to you to correct a great wrong. I will meet with your chiefs and medicine men." After saying his piece, he walked to the top of a grassy knoll outside the camp. A few minutes later the meeting took place on the knoll. Yaweta had never been told the name of the man he was after but it didn't take long to find him. When all were gathered he stood at the highest point and began to tell a story.

"An old man who has no name came to the door of my stronghold and camped many days seeking my help. He had his woman and his daughter with him. This was as it should be. The girl was in the flower of her youth and had never known a man. The nameless old man gave his daughter to me, Yaweta, as a sacrifice to right the wrong that was done to him. It has pleased me to call the girl Alzora because she has the beauty and grace of the fox. I have taken her to me as my woman. Now I am here to make an end to the wrong done to the man and punish the one who caused his trouble."

In response to the question voiced by the chief of the nation, "Who is this man?" Yaweta answered, "He is here sitting in this council". He told the story of how the old man had been betrayed and the sneak attack on the northern tribe. He ended by saying, "The killer of Big Tree is here." All the chiefs looked at one man. He was called Angry Bear. He rose to defend himself.

With great rhetoric Angry Bear claimed that the old man and his family were dead and Yaweta could not know these things. He thought he was making some headway with his silver tongue until the medicine man of his own tribe spoke up. He recalled some of the strange happenings of the time.

The chief claimed his right of trial by combat. Yaweta agreed even though the other chiefs thought the man had no right to fight a god. Angry Bear was so confident in his fighting ability that he was sure he would win, even against Yaweta. The weapons were knives and the fight was to be to the death.

His first lunge was his last but it was not fatal. Yaweta simply jumped back and kicked the knife out of his opponent's hand. Then he knocked his opponent off his feet by dropping to the ground and kicking his legs out from under him with a sweeping kick. Angry Bear hit the ground and Yaweta knelt on his chest. A steel knife was at Angry Bear's throat and the fight was over. Instead of killing, Yaweta tied the man and went back to conferring with the assembly. He said, "I am not the one to punish this one. He will be punished by those whom he has wronged so that all can see the justice of Yaweta".

The chief of all the tribes asked him to bring the old chief back to be honored and restored to his old office. Yaweta said they were now a part of the Redstone tribe and under his protection. He explained, "The Redstone are my special people. I am their protector and Alzora is their mother. Big Tree and his wife are the grandfather and grandmother of a great nation. In their troubles they have been honored above all. People of all nations and tribes who are homeless because of no fault of their own can come to me and, if they are worthy, I will make them a member. The Redstone will not fight unless attacked and will always help any tribe when they are needed." With this he showed them the symbol of the tribe and the ruby tipped arrows. "This is the mark of the Redstone. Honor this symbol and all will be well with you. I have bound the one who caused your war with the people to the north. I have defeated him in battle and his life is mine. There is a place between this camp and their camp. Meet me there when the sun rises two times. I will take one brave with me so he can come back and show you the place".

The scouts who brought Yaweta from the camp of the northern nation were sent back with the message. Yaweta camped about halfway between the two camps in a small valley. Two days later the chiefs, war chiefs, and medicine men of both nations gathered. The one who had caused all the trouble suffered a horrible death, before all, and peace was restored. Both tribes, in the next three days, learned all about the Redstone tribe that was not part of any nation.

Yaweta didn't mean it to happen, but in those nations, and all they contacted, the Redstone tribe had the reputation of being the children of a god of peace. The children of a good god like Yaweta would always be welcome. The symbol of the tribe would be recognized and honored.

Yaweta gathered ten strong braves from each of the nations and asked them to accompany him. He set the pace south at a steady lope. As they traveled the men with him were even more convinced that he could not be human. He never seemed to become tired. The braves felt that their legs would buckle under them and they would faint from lack of rest, food, and water, yet Yaweta kept moving. Yaweta's idea of a decent day's travel was twice as far as that of his companions.

At night he would bed down some distance from the others, partly because he preferred to be alone and partly because he never fully trusted the others. When the others bedded down for the night they could see Yaweta walking about or sitting quietly.   When   morning came he was always the one to wake the others. The braves began to wonder if Yaweta ever slept. One evening they began talking about it among themselves. After the big man had left the camp for his evening stroll they decided to find out for themselves.

Even as a young man In Erin, Sean had a second sense that told him when someone was near. Many times he had moved away just before the English discovered him. In this land that sense had become even more

199

developed. For most of his life Sean, now Yaweta had been a hunted man. Whenever he slept he was in grave danger. Before he married Alzora he had lain still as she got up from her pad on the floor and approached him. She would stand very still and watch him for several minutes. Then she would shiver slightly and quickly return to her bed. In spite of her shyness during the day he knew she loved him long before she was sure of the emotion herself.

Twenty different times different traveling companions came up to him in the night. Each time he waited until the man was close enough to hear him ask, in a low voice, "Why do you come to me so quietly in the night? Is something wrong in the camp? Do you wish to speak privately so that the others cannot hear?" The men with him were convinced that he never slept. Only a god could travel so far without being tired and then never sleep.

They were welcomed by all tribes until they got to the fierce tribes of the south. They were about to engage in battle when Yaweta was recognized. They had come into Apache territory, very close to the same route Yaweta had taken when he rode Lightning through the area. They were very close to the place where he had dispatched several braves that had mistaken him for an easy kill. A war party of nearly eighty braves was returning to their homes after a successful raid. They were full of the exuberance of victory and felt invincible. They charged down a hill toward Yaweta's band. They were within bowshot when the leader slid to a halt. Fear, surprise and even exuberance were in his voice as he called to his companions. In less than ten seconds the whole war party was going the other way. Two days later the travelers were attacked in quite a different way.

Over two hundred braves raced down another hill. This time the shouts had a different tone. Almost an arrow shot's distance ahead of the crowd was a brave almost as big as Yaweta. After a short visit with Sojata they proceeded on their way. Sojata was now supreme chief, so as long as they were in the tribe's territory they were protected and honored. The reputation of the Redstone tribe spread. His twenty companions were his best ambassadors.

They located the Cliff Dwellers in their new location, did their trading, and started the return journey to the north. On the way they stopped to get obsidian. All twenty men, and Yaweta, were carrying heavy loads when they deposited their burdens at the cliff trail. Yaweta didn't want the twenty braves going any farther. He gave each a gift of jewelry and thanked them for their help. Before beginning his work he made sure they had returned to their tribes. It took eighteen trips back and forth to bring everything down and through the tunnel. Only when this was done did he announce his return.

The next day Lightning carried the stores to the cave in three trips. It was good to be home. During the welcome feast he told the story of his adventure. Dad was happy that the family name had been exonerated but had no desire to return. The celebration lasted three days as Yaweta got acquainted with his family again. He had the distinct impression that the Indians he had met were under the illusion that the Redstone tribe was a lot bigger than six people.

Because of the amount of supplies obtained, it was ten peaceful years before another trip was made. Yaweta took his eldest son along on the next trip. He wanted to get him familiar with the trail and introduce him to the various tribes. It was a good trip. They were welcomed by all tribes and treated as honored guests.

Twice they helped in minor skirmishes and the young warrior became somewhat of a hero. At twelve summers he was as big and strong as any brave was, but had the recklessness of youth. This made him highly competitive.

While visiting with one of the tribes he wagered a handful of beads against an ax made of flint that he could catch and ride one of the big deer (the same animal we now call an Elk). He vowed to stay on its back until the count of ten.

The project took several days. Telia and several other young braves built a corral near a water hole and placed fresh cut grass in a large pile inside. The elk would come to drink and then graze a little. After a few days the animals became used to the coral and ignored it. One day a young bull elk entered to feed on the pile of hay. The boys quickly closed the gate. They finally caught the beast and Telia mounted it. It took three tries and caused some bruises before he was successful. The flint ax became his favorite weapon in hand-to-hand combat. It had a strong diamond willow handle and was expertly bound with strong rawhide. In one battle he killed six warriors with it. That was two more than any other brave.

Telia's meeting with Sojata, his half-brother, was memorial. Except for the age difference, it was as though Yaweta were looking at twins. Although their mothers were from different tribes, both men were of the same father. There was a strong family resemblance. For the next few weeks the brothers were never apart.

Yaweta met his grandchildren for the first time. It was evident that his genes were strong. His size, and his blue eyes, was even showing up in some of his grandchildren. Sojata had three fine sons and two beautiful daughters. They accompanied the travelers as far as the grave of the first Sojata. Then Yaweta and his young son continued on their journey. They were gone from the valley two winters.

Alzora became the mother of three more sons and two daughters. The tribe could not have been more contented. In this setting the first tragedy was experienced. On the event of the birth of the last child, Mom and Dad had moved in with the younger couple for a couple months. This was their usual custom. They helped with chores during the last month before the baby was born and for about a month afterward. It was toward the end of the winter months.

It became time for them to return home. Spring was on the way and a Chinook wind had blown for several hours. Their path took them close to the foot of a cliff. From high above the soil gave way beneath some boulders. The small avalanche took both their lives. If they had been much younger it would not have happened but they were not as agile as they were in their younger years. As near as Yaweta could tell they were in the neighborhood of eighty years of age. This was extremely long for anyone to live in that day.

Yaweta selected a grove of trees away from the caves and near the meadow. He built their platform and put them together so they would journey into the next life as a couple. It was a sad time for the Redstone tribe of nine living members. Yaweta reviewed their lives for all to hear. The oldest girl was appointed tribe scribe and recorded the history. He told briefly about their life before coming to the valley but went into detail about their roles as the grandfather and grandmother of the tribe. Their life story became a part of the history of the tribe.

28.
FAMILY

In the course of time Alzora presented her husband with a total of seven sons and five daughters. There were good times and bad. Some winters were harsh and there were some, where little snow fell. The years passed quickly and soon Yaweta's oldest son looked like a young duplicate of himself.

The young man had been getting restless so Yaweta sent him out to seek adventure. It was spring and Yaweta had not lived over fifty years without gaining some knowledge. He knew what was wrong with Telia even if the youngster didn't. He was to go visit the great Chief Sojata in the south, then trade with the Cliff Dwellers. All of Yaweta's sons had inherited the build, features, size, and blue eyes of their father. The strong family resemblance could not be missed.

Telia took two of his younger brothers with him. He had lived in the valley and seldom been out. There was that one time when he went with Yaweta and twice when they visited with the old tribe of his grandparents. The other two boys had never been farther than the cliff trail. It was time all three were on their own. Had they not moved to their own quarters across the valley and become braves?

By the time the three young braves found their half-brother, Sojata, they had helped four different tribes in battles. Once they helped a family out of the way of a stampede. They were like three young Yawetas and had gained reputations of their own. After a month with Chief Sojata, their education was much farther advanced. In all things they conducted themselves as representatives of their tribe and all it meant.

After visiting with the Cliff Dwellers, and going to the memorial of the first Sojata, the trio headed north, knowing a whole lot more about their father. They agreed together to learn much more, so instead of going right home with their burdens of turquoise they decided to go another way. They stopped to pick up some of the obsidian and then headed northeast toward the settlement of the descendants of the crew of the Dame Mary.

They arrived late in the year, just in time to help with the annual hunt. It was an experience they never forgot. They found that many of the tribe called Mandan spoke the same tongue as the Redstone official language. By talking to the elders, they learned much more about Yaweta's past. They accepted an invitation to spend the winter with the tribe. Their hut was built on the outer edge of the village and was made of sod.

In the early part of the winter the tribe was attacked. They were raiders from the north who lived by the spoils of war. The Mandan were seldom attacked so they had lost some of their skill in the battlefield. The raiders made one mistake. Their attack started between the brothers' home and the main village. They had either overlooked or discounted that one hut. The three young Yawetas led a surprising counterattack from the rear. By the time the raiders were beaten off they had sustained heavy losses. Over fifty braves had started out and one could count the survivors with his fingers. The Mandan tribe suffered two losses. A brave and his wife had been away from the camp near the river when they were jumped by the raiders. They left a family.

The three Redstone natives had befriended that family. There were two daughters, Blue Sky and Star Child, and three sons. The friendship had something to do with Telia's interest in Blue Sky and the obvious eyes his brother Sawatago had for Star Child. Both Telia and

Sawatago were past the age that most braves were married. The three boys of the family had not yet become braves and had been orphans that the older couple adopted. Blue Sky had just celebrated the tribe's ritual of womanhood that declared her available for marriage. Three braves had brought gifts but they were refused.

Young Telia was happy that her father had seen fit to leave her uncommitted. In the celebration that followed the battle the men were offered the gratitude of the tribe and the chief asked what he could do for them. Telia said they would not accept anything but he would like to have Blue Sky for his wife if she was agreeable. When she ran from the women who stood outside the circle listening to the men talk and jumped into his arms he assumed she was agreeable. Another wild celebration started immediately.

The marriage ceremony was performed within a month. It was then he discovered that he had not only gotten a bride. He was now responsible for the whole family. Sawatago seemed pleased and so did Star Child. The three young boys ran to all their friends, bragging. When the whole group left for the valley the next spring Telia wondered what Yaweta would say. He had no need to worry.

On the journey across the plains they captured six buffalo calves - one male and five females. Telia had a plan for them and determined to bring them into the valley. They were difficult to handle for a while but training and patience paid off. By the time they reached the river and headed south the calves were carrying some of the burdens.

Two days before they got to the cliff trail the youngest Redstone was sent ahead, to announce their arrival. He was the most fleet of foot in the group. By the time the party got to the cliff trail Yaweta and Alzora were waiting. The first thing Yaweta noticed about Blue Sky was the color of her eyes. Her name suited her. Her eyes were sky blue. Both girls' eyes were blue and their skin was much lighter than most Indians were. Yaweta knew where his sons had been without asking. He was anxious for any news.

Getting the calves across the cliff trail was difficult. One of them fell and would have been lost if it had not had a leather rope tied to it. The pack and animal were saved but it suffered a broken leg. The calf was the main course at the feast, welcoming the wanderers back and greeting the new tribal members. It was a feast of joy in the valley.

The newlyweds took over the cave of their grandparents. The young boys built a Hogan nearby and two months later Sawatago and Star Child made ready another cave. They were married about the time of the first snows. The calves grew and became both beasts of burden and producers of meat for the tribe.

One evening Telia and Blue Sky came to visit. They announced the expected birth of the first grandchild. The important second generation of the Redstone tribe was on the way. Blue Sky told of a promise she had made her grandfather. If her first child was a boy she had promised to name it Sean, after a friend of her grandfather. Normally, the father picks a name for his children and she had said as much. Her grandfather had told her that if she was as pretty as he expected her to be it would be easy to persuade her husband. She was and it was. Yaweta asked her grandfather's name. She only knew his Indian name.

The description matched that of the youngest regular member of the old crew. He was a young man, about ten years older than Yaweta, with blonde hair and a strange name. It was Sven, the Scott with a Scandinavian father. Yaweta had hit it off well with Sven because of their shared youth and he was the only one who even came close in strength. It was decided the child would be named Sean, if it was a boy, after Yaweta told his son the truth about the name.

29.
THE YAWETAS

After the first grandchild was born the tribe seemed to grow rapidly. Other sons went out for adventure and brought back brides. Some never returned. They were killed in some manner or another or found another life. The three boys that Telia adopted grew and took three of Yaweta's daughters as wives. The other two girls went out with their brothers and returned with young braves of their choosing. It seemed as though only a little time had passed before the valley had a substantial community living in the forest and caves. Some even chose to live outside of the valley in the basin on the other side of the tunnel. Twenty years passed quickly for Yaweta.

Young men dream and act on their dreams. Old men have visions and tell about them. Yaweta became a very old man. Technically, he was still the head of the tribe, but most of the duties of The Yaweta had passed to Telia. Yaweta was held in deep regard as the father of the tribe but the young braves looked to the son for guidance in most matters. When Telia talked to his father he expressed his concern that this was happening. Yaweta told him it was as it should be. Old things must pass away and new things come to life. "Look to the forests and the meadows. In winter everything dies to all appearances, but each spring new life replaces the old. It is the same with our tribe. The tribe will not die but the leaders will change. It is time to change".

It was early in the spring when he called the tribe together. He had the women prepare a feast in the meadow near the lake. The preparations took several days even with everyone helping. The entire tribe met, dressed in their best attire, for the ceremony everyone knew was about to take place. After the first meal Yaweta got up to speak. He told of a dream he had been having.

He dreamed he was on the mountain near the entrance to the valley. There was a brilliant light and a golden path appeared. He walked up the path toward the sky and into a bright light. He saw his mother and father waiting for him and Alzora was by his side. Even his son of many years ago was there. Sojata came to him dressed in elegant white clothing and wearing a golden headdress. In the dream he was about to embrace the Great Spirit in the form of a man when he was told that the time had not yet come but it would be soon. He was told to return and finish his life's work. It was then Yaweta woke.

He said he had been told to give his son the title of Yaweta. With this he called Telia up and presented him with the gold necklace of leadership. "This is the symbol of the sun which will always shine, golden, in the sky above the valley". Then he took the original emblem of the tribe that he had made with his own hands. "This is the flag of the tribe and always rests over the heart of its people. The flag must never leave the valley but the symbol must be carried over the heart, in pride, wherever the members of the tribe travel".

Yaweta spoke of the beginning and the high purpose of its people. He spoke of the adversity that started the tribe and the deep sorrow that other tribes had caused their own people. He asked the assembly to vow never to become so self-important that they could not reach out to others in need. It was not a reaching down to others, but a reaching out. No person was beneath another so it would never be necessary to reach down.

Yaweta continued by asking the people to follow his son as they had followed him. With this the people stood and cheered their agreement. When things calmed down Yaweta said. "From this moment on you are no longer Telia. This name can be given to another. Your name is now Yaweta, and all who speak to you must call you by this name. For the short time I still walk the earth I will be known as Father." From the time that he first became, "Yaweta" until the time that he gave up the name was just short of eighty years. He was indeed a very old man.

The transfer of leadership of all Redstone Indians was completed and the celebration continued in honor of the new Yaweta.

A week later the man who was called Father went up the side of the mountain to the place he had been inspired to create the emblem. He sat and waited. It was during the height of the sun when lightning struck the spot. The new Yaweta and his mother, Alzora, witnessed the event, as did with many of the tribe. There was not a cloud in the sky, yet there was lightning. Some swore they had seen his face in the lightning and saw him go up with the streak of fire into the sky.

There was a burned place on the ground but not a trace of the man that had been standing there. Alzora, upon realizing her Yaweta was gone, collapsed. As she lay on the ground her right arm went out and her hand closed as though she were holding hands with someone. She spoke her parent's names and then turned her head toward the right and smiled. A spark appeared in her eyes and slowly faded as she left her body.

The tribe fasted for three days, weeping openly. The cries of mourning could be heard throughout the valley and to the basin beyond. Every man stood before the tribe and told all they knew about their founders. Alzora was placed on the highest platform and honored. A month later the new Yaweta moved his family into the cave with the room of lights. The next day he called the tribe together and exhorted them to give up their sorrow and live as they felt the first Yaweta would want.

Generations passed and the Red Stone tribe became everything the first Yaweta had wanted. They were the peacemakers between warring tribes. The Yaweta of the Redstone became the final authority in disputes between tribes, and in many instances advised the chiefs of nations. A conference ground was established on the edge of the plateau where the cliff trail started.

The tribal population stabilized itself between two hundred and two hundred and fifty. The normal passing of people because of age and accidents accounted for much of the lack of growth. Many left to seek adventure and some never returned. A few were banished because they had done something against the tribe's laws but did not deserve death. Always, the tribe's symbol was honored and the principals it represented. Not one Redstone Indian brought dishonor upon the tribe. It seemed to be a voluntary prerequisite to remove the symbol and leave the tribe when an individual had reservations about the tribe's laws and traditions.

Nearly fifteen Yaweta's had ruled the tribe before the first white man was reported. At first, reports came from the braves who had traveled south. The Cliff Dwellers had disappeared but their craft was practiced by others. The first reports were of men wearing armor and carrying spears and swords. Some of them rode strange animals. Others carried a stick that belched flame and smoke and killed at a great distance without being thrown. The strangers did not want to talk. They pointed their sticks when they saw the party and the sticks killed one of their numbers. A hole appeared in the chest of one of the braves and he fell dead.

Later reports were of a different kind of white man. This one dressed in robes of a strange material and carried no weapons. He spoke kindly in sign language and welcomed all people in peace. They called themselves priests. When the party of Redstone Indians first contacted the peaceful white men there was no communication, other than in sign language. Then one evening one of the priests overheard two of the braves talking in the Redstone language. Both the natives and the priest were equally surprised when the priest spoke Gaelic. He was from Ireland.

The priest thought, at first, that a miracle had happened. When he understood that it was the language of the tribe, he wondered at their origins. He wrote of the discovery in his report to his superiors but none of them believed him.

In later years when the Mandan tribe was discovered to have had Scottish ancestors it was thought that the braves were of the Mandan tribe. The references to the Redstone Tribe in different writings were thought to be another part of, or name for, the Mandan tribe. It never occurred to historians that there could be two tribes with Gaelic origins.

The braves spent a year helping the priests learn some of the languages of the natives and learning about the white man. Eventually they were introduced to some of the soldiers from Spain. It was a full year before they started back to the valley. They looked forward to making their report to the Yaweta and the tribe. Upon hearing their story, the Yaweta sent his oldest son to learn about the white man and his culture. When he became Yaweta he would need to know all about the new people. The son carried the name of one of the most honored of all names. His name was Sojataha, which could be translated to mean Son of the Giant Protector of the People's Ghost.

Sojataha and three companions arrived at the pueblo of the priest. There was a sickness the priest called smallpox affecting the entire population of Indians. Sojataha and his friends helped care for the victims for several days before he sent his friends back to the valley to get them away from the infection. He told them they needed more help from the Redstone tribe.

Eventually, Sojataha came down with the ailment and spent long hours delirious with fever. He was big like many of his ancestors and had the blue eyes that had become a trademark of the Redstone tribe. There was enough of the sturdy blood of his ancestors to fight the disease and eventually he recovered but he had no memory of the past. The fever had taken his heritage from him.

The three braves Sojataha sent back rode the animals the white man called horses. It was a much faster mode of travel and before long they could ride easily while the horses ran. They had been gone several days when the first one started getting weak. A few days later the second one came down with the smallpox. In his turn the third started showing symptoms. By the time he arrived at the cliff trail he was the only survivor and very weak. He was carried over the cliff trail and into the valley.

The women bathed him in the lake in an effort to bring down his fever. He could barely talk and when he did his words made no sense to the tribe. He kept saying one word, "smallpox". They had never heard the word before and did not understand its significance. He died three days later and was put on his platform. Before long several members of the tribe were sick.

One by one they fell to the disease. The Yaweta, and those who were able, took care of the sick and buried the dead. Burial platforms were hanging in trees all over the valley and even in the area between the tunnel and the cliff trail. Every night the Yaweta went down to the room of lights and soaked in the warm water of the pool before sleeping. Every morning he went out to find that more of his tribe had passed away during the darkness.

Within a month the Yaweta built the last platform. The Redstone tribe no longer lived. He was weak with the sickness when he built his own platform and waited to die. He climbed up and lay down expecting life to leave him at any time. The tribe, by tradition, buried the Yaweta near the mountain away from the regular burying grounds. It was a way of honoring their leaders. This is where he had built his platform knowing that when his son returned he would look for his father there.

He slept. Rain was falling in his face and he was hungry. He did not know how long he had been on the platform but he knew he was alive. He found food and ate. He thought that there had to have been a purpose for his survival. The Redstone tribe was not dead as long as he was alive.

The stench of the dead was heavy in the air. He determined to move all the belongings of the dead to the burial grounds of the people. In so doing he eliminated all trace of their existence, reasoning that one day a new beginning would start and the old would, of necessity, be forgotten. In the words of his ancestor, the tribe was in its winter. He believed his son would return and a new beginning would bring forth life.

The last of his job finished, he went to his cave and down to the room of lights. During the night a lightning storm came and a fire was started. He did not

215

hear the lightning or smell the smoke because he was sleeping beside the pool. The fire burned the burial place completely consuming everything. As often happens during such storms a heavy rain fell on part of the forest while the rest burned. Most of the trees were saved because of the rain and a strong wind that blew from the south toward the north. The fire started spreading through the grass of the meadow. When the Yaweta came out of his cave in the morning the whole meadow was on fire. Rain came again and the fire was extinguished but over half of the valley was destroyed.

The lightning storm that started the fire in the valley also started one on the other side of the tunnel. Most of the forest from the creek to the cliff trail was burned. A few of the bigger trees survived but almost everything else was gone. The Yaweta looked on it as a cleansing of the land for a new generation by the Great Spirit. The smell of burned grass and wood was a lot more pleasant than the smell of the dead.

Winter came early and stayed late. Snow was deep in the valley, preventing the Yaweta from hunting. He was forced to eat the last of Buffalo. He recorded the history of the tribe in pictographs along the walls of the tunnel and in the cave during the winter months. He had always liked making pictures to tell stories and he thought these would be better than the written word because anyone could understand them.

When the snow finally left and spring came the grass sprang forth through the blackened remains of the fire. It was thicker than ever and soon covered the meadow with green. A profusion of color sprinkled the meadow as wild flowers bloomed in the rippling sea of grass. The willows along the creek began to grow back with vigor. Out of the ashes of destruction sprang forth-new life. The Yaweta saw it as a prediction of new life for the tribe.

He seemed to have a purpose to his existence. Something drove him to preserve the history on the walls, yet make the valley clean as though preparing for a new civilization. He removed all signs of the old and waited for the new. The motivation was strong within him and he began to have glimpses of forgotten visions. He had planned to pass his title to his son on the return of his visit with the white priests but five years passed and his son, Sojataha, never returned. After thirty winters as the leader he felt tired and wanted to retire. Now his energy was revitalized toward something new but he knew not what new thing was coming.

He prepared for future trade by spending long hours making arrowheads, spear points, and beads. The urns were almost full and lined up near the door of the room of lights. All was prepared for a new beginning and the energy in his body began to subside. He dreamed nearly every night of the valley as it appeared before man had entered.

A new dream came to him. For seven nights he had the same vision. He had become very old and knew his time was short so the dreams did not disturb him. He saw himself in the burial platform he had built but it was much higher as though he were a great chief. The Great Spirit appeared above him, welcoming him home. Beside the Great Spirit stood the first Yaweta, his wife Alzora, and the first Sojata. He saw the other Yawetas standing together and greeting him. He had known one of the other Yawetas, but had never seen any of the others. Somehow he knew each of them.

In the seventh dream he heard a voice say, "It is time". The next morning he placed his platform higher in the tree in accordance with his dream. He removed the sign of his existence from the cave and surrounding area. His last act was to paint the last pictograph depicting his own death. He was very weak and could barely climb to the platform. He wore the Yaweta's necklace and carried with him arrows and a spear. On his chest he placed the emblem, the flag of the nation that the first Yaweta had made. He did all this in accordance to the dream.

As he laid waiting for his spirit to leave him he dreamed again. He was assured that the tribe was not dead. Many years would pass but one would come who was worthy and the tribe would live again. In the distant future a descendent of Yaweta would come and the tribe would become even more powerful than ever. With this assurance calmness came over him. The last Yaweta joined the Yawetas that had come before him to live with the Great Spirit and watch over the valley.

www.ingramcontent.com/pod-product-compliance
Lightning Source LLC
Chambersburg PA
CBHW072052170626
46813CB00004B/1322